CU00835782

The
and
Tribulations
of
Arkwright and Doris Broughton

To: Cornforth & Cornforth

The Trials
and
Tribulations
of
Arkwright and Doris Broughton

For John to read & for Viv to colour in the pictures.

Alan Booth

With best wishes

(ALAN BOOTH)

27 August 2005

The Pentland Press Limited
Edinburgh • Cambridge • Durham • USA

© Alan Booth 2000

First published in 2000 by
Alan Booth
83 Rickmansworth Road
Watford
Herts WD1 7JB

This novel is a work of fiction. Names and characters are the
product of the author's imagination and any resemblance to actual
persons, living or dead, is entirely coincidental.

All rights reserved.
Unauthorised duplication
contravenes existing laws.

British Library Cataloguing in Publication Data.
A Catalogue record for this book is available
from the British Library.

ISBN 1 85821 760 1

Typeset by CBS, Martlesham Heath, Ipswich, Suffolk
Printed and bound by Antony Rowe Ltd., Chippenham

To my wife Valerie, and my son Richard,
and in remembrance of my
Mother and Father.

Contents

Foreword

For Arkwright and Doris Broughton, pillars of the community in the small sleepy village of Clapthorn in Widdledale, (somewhere in Yorkshire), life is uncomplicated. That is – until they are sent by their local branch of the National Farmers' Union to visit the ranch of Wilbur and Mary-Lou Jackson in America. Their trip is terminated abruptly by a tornado which devastates the ranch and propels Wilbur into outer space.

Shortly after Doris and Arkwright return home, Old Tom Bones shuffles off his mortal coil. When his Last Will and Testament is published, his 'woman what did for him' whilst he was alive is more than a bit put out when she discovers that she had not been remembered by Old Tom. The villagers are also surprised to find that little Bessie Sidebottom was also not remembered – but that surprise is as of nothing when it is disclosed that Old Tom has left his entire estate to Doris for a past service rendered to him.

Doris disappears to London and Seth Womersley (self-proclaimed ace investigative reporter of the *Widdledale Gazette*) traces her to her secret location.

The key to the mystery of what happened between Old Tom and Doris Broughton is contained in Old Tom's diaries – but these have gone missing. Constable Pixter is put on the case until Mr Blenkin finds him in a seemingly compromising position with his wife. The police inquiries are handed over to PC Wellbeloved who ultimately discovers the location of the diaries – not least of all through the assistance of Mrs Troughton, who sees all that goes on in the village from her lounge window.

An arrest is made for the theft of the diaries – but not before the culprit commits two acts of violence against the police and has to spend an uncomfortable few hours in the cells of Wellerby police station.

It is left to Mr Grimsdyke, the local bank manager (Old Tom's executor), and to Mr Ben Driglington (Old Tom's solicitor) to reveal the truth about Old Tom Bones and Doris.

As one person leaves the village it is open for another to appear.

Chapter 1

A Load of Hot Air

Arkwright Broughton and his wife Doris sat huddled over their coal fire. The Yorkshire Dale, where Arkwright had a small farm, was an inhospitable place in the middle of winter. But this year the winter seemed to trouble them less than in previous years.

It was about a month ago that Arkwright had told Doris he was off to the Annual General Meeting of the Widdledale Branch of the National Farmers' Union. Normally, Arkwright declined to attend the AGM in case he should suddenly find himself elected onto the committee – as had happened seven years ago when he had fallen asleep during its proceedings. However, this year – as a precautionary measure – he had taken a nap in the afternoon and had concluded that, in a refreshed state, it would be safe for him to attend. 'Any road,' as Arkwright was later to tell folk, 'I went.'

And it was fortuitous that he did go, for – to cut a long story short – he found himself chosen to go on an exchange (with Doris) to a ranch in America.

When Arkwright got home from his meeting and had told Doris that they were yankee doodle land bound, she just didn't believe him. He might just as well have told her that they had been chosen for a trip to the moon.

'America! Oh my! America!' Doris kept saying. 'Do they speak English there?'

'They do their best,' Arkwright replied.

'Have you ever noticed,' Doris asked. 'in the war films we see at the cinema, the American soldiers are always running?'

'Happen it's because they're allus late to join the war,' Arkwright suggested. 'Anyhow, there'll be no wars going on round the ranch we'll be stopping at, so we shalln't have to take us running shoes with us. Do yer think I'd best get one of those cowboy hats to go with, or shall I just tek me flat cap?'

Arkwright was very fond of his flat cap. On very cold nights he had been known to wear it in bed.

'Aye, tek thee flat cap, it'll look right gradely over there,' said Doris – secretly hoping it would get lost at some stage on the trip.

Now *going abroad* for Doris and Arkwright had previously meant an expedition from their village of Clapthorn to Wellerby, the small market town about twenty miles up the road. Arkwright had occasionally ventured further afield – such as when he went over the top to a show in the next Dale but, for Doris, the nearest she had ever been to foreign parts was a solitary day trip with the Mothers' Union to Bridlington. And now, here she was, going to America.

Doris did fret a little as to where they'd catch the bus in Wellerby as she'd never seen one with America written on its destination board.

'Nay, lass,' Arkwright told her, 'we have to fly there and we'll need those things called passports.'

Fortunately for the pair of innocents, all the administrative details for their trip were taken care of by that nice young Mr Blair from the National Farmers' Union. The only point of contention was that they would have to fly to America from Manchester Airport – and Manchester was in Lancashire.

'Bah gum! Lancashire!' Arkwright said with the horror of one who had been asked to betray King and Country.

On the appointed day, a limousine from Harry Robertshaw's fleet of taxis came to take the intrepid travellers to the airport. The cars were mainly used for weddings and funerals and, as befits such occasions, the cars had a certain style about them. Arkwright and Doris felt like royalty as they waved a temporary farewell to the cluster of good folk of Clapthorn who had assembled at the gates to their farm to wish them *bon voyage*.

Thus it was that in the summer of '97 Arkwright and Doris were

2

on the ranch of Wilbur and Mary-Lou Jackson. Everything in America seemed very big to Arkwright and Doris – not least of all, the mouths of their hosts.

'On my ranch,' Wilbur boasted to Arkwright, 'I can get up with the sun and ride my horse til the sun sets and still not have reached the edge of my ranch.'

'Aye, lad,' said Arkwright, 'I once had hoss like that.'

On most days Wilbur showed Arkwright over his ranch and introduced him to pieces of machinery he had never imagined possible. Doris, during these times, went to down-town Bushville with Mary-Lou to explore the shops and to spend some of the money that Arkwright had loaned her at a nominal rate of interest.

At evening time the men and women came together for dinner which, as often as not, was a barbecue. Eating the main meal of the day *alfresco* style was something of an experience for Arkwright. Of course, as a boy, he'd enjoyed picnics in the meadow and in the woods – and they were all right. But the idea of cooking and eating every dinner outside was, he thought, a step backwards in time.

Doris could tell what Arkwright was thinking and, giving him one of her looks, said, 'Barbecues are very popular these days in Harrogate and we have to keep up with the trends.'

'Harrogate? Harrogate?' thundered Arkwright. 'That's not a place with proper people. Them posh lot there get dressed up and have a band in just for the opening of an envelope.' Arkwright had never actually been to Harrogate, but he'd heard tell of it.

Arkwright had just got the women organised to do the clearing up after the day's 'barby' when he saw, out of the corner of his eye, something odd in the distance.

'Aye up lad,' said Arkwright to Wilbur, 'what's that over there?'

Wilbur turned to look in the direction Arkwright was pointing and went pale. The swirling object was moving steadily towards the two men and they could both see it sucking up objects in its path.

But before Arkwright could say to Wilbur that he'd better peg the old woman down or there'd be nobody to do the tidying up later, Wilbur had cut a solitary dash to his car, jumped in it and driven off at speed. About a mile down the road his progress was unexpectedly

3

impeded by a cow falling from the sky and depositing itself in front of his car. The bovine appeared to be no less confused than Wilbur at this sudden turn of events in their respective lives. As Wilbur got out of the car for a closer inspection of the scene, a sudden gust of wind blew him into the powerful suck of the tornado.

At the sight of Wilbur now in the middle distance, twisting and twirling upwards and onwards, Arkwright stood dumbstruck. He was horrified at the damage being inflicted on the ranch but took comfort from the fact that it was not his farm being devastated so disastrously. As the tornado approached him, his thoughts, unlike those of Wilbur, turned to procuring the safety of Doris, Mary-Lou and (especially) himself. If he didn't look sharp, they would all be joining Wilbur in the great beyond.

Now by happy chance, Doris was a person of substantial proportions – but having seen the tornado in the distance lift up whole sheds he knew he needed more than her as an anchor. He got the three of them into the cupboard under the stairs of the Jackson homestead and made sure that Doris was positioned firmly against the door. Then they waited for the tornado to reach them.

A sudden *whoosh* took the roof off the house and the contents of the bedrooms received a dramatic and early spring clean. But the cupboard under the stairs held out to be a safe haven.

When it seemed that the danger had passed, the trio emerged from their shelter to survey the damage wreaked by the tornado.

'They don't have breezes like that where I come from,' Arkwright commented to Mary-Lou as she stood contemplating the departure of the upper part of her home and, of course, Wilbur.

Several days later the remnants of the house were found some fifteen or so miles away – but of Wilbur there was no trace. 'Happen the lad's gone to heaven, he was heading in that direction last time a I saw him,' Arkwright suggested to Mary-Lou. She was as unconvinced as she was unconsoled by Arkwright's words of intended comfort.

All in all, it seemed appropriate to Arkwright and Doris that they should not create a fuss about their holiday being spoiled but, rather, take an early departure from their one remaining host. With thanks for a truly memorable holiday, Arkwright and Doris bade a fond farewell of Mary-Lou. Arkwright – in a parting message – said that his solicitor would be writing to her about his compensation claim for trauma if she would be so kind as to forward her new address to him as soon as possible.

On his return home Arkwright dutifully reported back to the NFU. He told them that he didn't understand what a tornado was but it had been explained to him that it was a load of hot air. 'Whatever it were,' he told the assembled farmers, 'it were a right to-do, were that.' And it was a story which was to earn him the price of many a jar of ale at the Cat and Fiddle when he related his tale to visitors to the Dales. The way Arkwright told it made the *Rime of the Ancient Mariner* look like bedtime story for a two-year-old.

Mary-Lou Jackson, Arkwright and Doris watch the tornado

Chapter 2

A Dying Business

'In the good old days,' Arkwright Broughton bemoaned to his wife Doris, 'when you died and did it proper you got the Co-op to see you into the ground and do a nice ham and tongue tea for those who'd taken the trouble to come and see you off.' Whilst he did not articulate the point on this occasion, Arkwright had often been known to comment that it was a comfort to be in the sure and certain knowledge that, whatever the cost of your being put away by the Co-op, the divi was still accruing after you had gone.

'These days,' Arkwright protested to Doris, 'it's a fifteen minute affair at the crematorium with your coffin placed on some clanking mechanical contraption which hasn't had chance to get cold from conveying the last body to the fiery furnace – and when you look behind you as you go out there's another lot moving into the pews you've just left. If that's what dying has come to,' Arkwright expounded, 'then I think it's grossly overrated.'

Most of the village had turned out for the funeral of Old Tom Bones and those who hadn't actually made it to the crematorium had managed to make an early claim to the most favourable seats at the Cat and Fiddle where food was being set out for the hungry returning mourners.

As an act of kindness, Arkwright and Doris had taken Miss Price with them to the service. Miss Price was ninety-five years of age and fast failing in health. However, notwithstanding her terminal infirmities, having grown up with Old Tom she had been anxious to be with him as he made his last appearance in village society. As

6

Arkwright looked at her frail and shaking form he couldn't help but contemplate that simple economics suggested it would be cheaper all round if he just left her propped up in the chapel at the end of the service. But it was an idea he didn't dare to suggest to Doris.

Arkwright and his party were the last of the mourners to arrive at the Cat and Fiddle. Their journey back from the crematorium – some forty miles away – had been slow as they had been obliged to impose themselves on the generous nature and facilities of the good folk of the Dale every five or six miles so that Miss Price could relieve her discomfiture. 'Funerals always have this effect on me,' Miss Price said by way of explanation and apology to Arkwright and Doris. *I know one which won't,* was a thought Arkwright kept to himself in the interests of good taste.

Old Tom had been something of a fixture at the Cat and Fiddle for upwards of seventy years and it had been known for some months that he had left a tidy sum of money behind the bar so the village could celebrate when the great landlord in the sky had shouted 'Time' for him. 'Celebrate' was the word Old Tom had used because he saw shuffling off his mortal coil as a necessary step to his entrance into the next world where, he was convinced, there was a pub on the corner of every cloud and opening hours were unrestricted.

By the time Arkwright and his party entered the pub all the seats were taken but with much a to-do and rearrangement of human forms, places were found for the two ladies. One seat, though, remained unoccupied – that which had taken the frame of Old Tom over so many years. Nobody thought it right to take up his seat next to the fire on this, his special day.

Having to stand gave Arkwright a prominent position in the room from which he could speak down to those sitting at the tables. 'The problem with dying,' he said, 'is that you feel very stiff the following day. It'll happen to us all one day and when I go I don't want any fuss or bother.'

'Right then,' said Doris, a tad too speedily, thought Arkwright.

Before Arkwright could elaborate on what he had actually meant by 'no fuss and bother', the conversation had moved on to an indecent discussion of the disposal of Old Tom's worldly goods.

7

'He must have been worth a bob or two and he didn't have any family, did he?' Mrs Oglethorpe pronounced rather than asked. Turning to Mr Grimsdyke, the local Bank manager sitting next to her, she asked with characteristic bluntness, as to how much he thought the estate would be worth and whether he had any knowledge of the deceased's testamentary bequests. Mrs Oglethorpe had been Old Tom's 'woman what does' for nearly twenty years and, like young Pip, she had 'great expectations'.

Mr Grimsdyke was not about to let any indiscretions slip from his lips – even though he was acutely aware that when the Will became public knowledge not a few eyebrows would be raised.

It was indeed true that Old Tom had money. He had inherited a sizeable farm from his father to which he had added several hundreds of acres over the years – the funding of which additions had always been something of a mystery to the village folk. When, in turn, Old Tom had retired, the farm had been sold – and whilst the amount had never become public knowledge, it was the talk of the Dale that Old Tom had become exceedingly rich.

Although Old Tom had never been considered 'near', he was not known for careless spending. He had given generously when funds were needed for the repair of the village hall and he never failed to stand his round at the Cat and Fiddle. However, he had always let it be known that he had 'certain responsibilities' without ever explaining what these might be and had, as a consequence, to exercise a good measure of prudence in his financial affairs.

And now at the time of his departure there were not a few in the village who were hoping that his sense of 'responsibility' might have been extended to them.

Major Jack Bones, TD (no relation, and absentee Lord of the Manor) had long sought, via extensive correspondence, to persuade Old Tom to give financial backing to his scheme for 'The Bones' Handicap' to be instituted at either the Ripon or Thirsk racecourses. The Major was aware of Old Tom's keen interest in the gee-gees and had advanced the idea that the naming of such a handicap would be a lasting memorial to Old Tom's interest in the sport of kings. When Old Tom had, in turn, directly addressed to him the point that this might more reflect permanent glory on the Major rather than on himself, the Major had replied saying the thought had never crossed his mind.

Another with high hopes was little Bessie Sidebottom who, if rumours were to be believed, had offered comfort and aid to Old Tom beyond the normal course of duties of a neighbour. At one time, little Bessie had suddenly left the village 'to go and look after a dying aunt' and at the time of her departure she was, some said, fuller in figure than was normal for a single lady. Speculation continued after her return some months later when she certainly looked much slimmer.

But little Bessie, the Major and other hopefuls were going to have to wait.

It was about a fortnight after the funeral that Mr Ben Driglington (Old Tom's solicitor) arrived at the home of Old Tom together with Mr Grimsdyke, the Executor of the estate. A large removal van arrived shortly afterwards and the contents of Old Tom's house were removed and driven away. A day later an estate agent's board announced that the house was for sale.

In due course the house was sold and still the final affairs of Old Tom remained a mystery to the village.

It's not that country folk are overly obsessed with the affairs of other people, but the unpleasant rumours and speculation going the rounds were such that Arkwright thought he should take some lead in the matter. He therefore took it upon himself to call upon Mr Grimsdyke to see if some statement might be made so that the memory of Old Tom could be freed from all the unseemly gossip which was circulating. It was a surprise to Arkwright to see Doris walking out of Mr Grimsdyke's office as he was awaiting his call to the inner sanctum.

Before he could ask Doris what was afoot, he was ushered into the manager's office.

'Why's Doris been to see thee?' he asked of Mr Grimsdyke, only to be told that the affairs of a customer could not be discussed with another person – even if that person was her husband. It was not an answer Arkwright was happy to accept – but to accept it he had. His immediate reaction was to chase after Doris demanding explanations

9

but Mr Grimsdyke held Arkwright with his eye and asked the purpose of the visit.

Arkwright said he knew the Manager must be aware of things which were being circulated in the village about Old Tom and asked why he couldn't say something to put an end to the rumours. Mr Grimsdyke heaved a deep sigh and said he could say nothing other than that details of the Will would appear in the local press the following day.

Much concerned about Doris' visit to the Bank, Arkwright made a speedy return to his home – but when he arrived there was no sign of Doris, only a note saying that she would be away for a couple of days.

Now Arkwright was not a man made in the modern mould and Doris' actions smacked to him of downright insubordination. She hadn't even sided the breakfast dishes. But not knowing where she had gone, there was little he could do about the matter – the dishes could wait until she returned. He did consider ringing round family and friends to see if any of them knew where Doris was, but he didn't do so for fear of the shame of it. He battened down the hatches to await her return, only stepping out the following day to get his copy of the local paper. And there it was on the front page:

'Doris Broughton had love child by Old Tom.'

Chapter 3

Where's Doris?

The medicinal brandy had been brought out of the sideboard and was being downed by Arkwright Broughton in inebriate proportions. It was beyond his immediate comprehension that the lower proportions of his wife's body had, at some time in the past, heaved too and fro in unison with those of the late Old Tom Bones.

The very thought of it sickened him. Leastwise, he now knew why his wife, Doris, had done a flit from the family homestead. 'Family homestead,' he said aloud to himself. 'I can't call it that any more.'

Now had it been that Bill Clinton chap in America who he'd read about in the papers and seen on the television, it would have been a different matter. The President of the United States of America tumbling his wife was one thing; having it done by Old Tom was another.

There was a knock on Arkwright's front door. For a few moments he debated as to whether or not to respond to it. But in the end curiosity got the better of him.

He opened the door and was momentarily blinded by the flash of a camera. 'Whom are you?' demanded Arkwright who had once attended evening classes in English Language. 'And put that bloody camera away.'

The cameraman stood back to make way for Seth Womersley, the reporter from the *Widdledale Gazette*. 'Can we have a word with Mrs Broughton?' he enquired.

The question posed something of a dilemma for Arkwright.

11

One the one hand, he couldn't say that Doris was upstairs in bed and on the other couldn't say she was out shopping. Furthermore, and quite forgetting the number hands appended to the human body, he didn't want to say that she had 'done a bunk'. In the confusion of the moment he told the reporter that she had 'done a bonk.'

'Yes, we know all about that, Mr Arkwright,' said Seth. 'That's what we're here to talk to Mrs Broughton about.'

'Nay lad,' said Arkwright, 'you're getting me all confused. She's done a bunk. She's gone off and I don't know where. She left me a note saying she was going away for a couple of days.'

'I suppose you've read in the Gazette that she's inherited three million pounds from Old Tom for having his baby?' Seth asked.

Arkwright, not one usually prone to public displays of emotion, suddenly found tears streaming down his face. His vision, though, was not so impaired that he didn't see the press photographer levelling his camera at him again.

'I warned thee once lad about that camera,' Arkwright said and, with a sudden lunge, he snatched the camera, threw it to the ground and stamped heavily on it. 'Sue me if you like and I'll have you before the Press Complaints body before you can say 'Instamatic'.' The photographer surveyed with disbelief the parts of his camera spilled out before him.

Before he could begin to think how he was going to explain to the Editor the loss of the *Gazette*'s only camera, Arkwright had pointed him in the direction of a dustpan and brush and told him to get the mess cleared up. And for good measure he told him to get the breakfast dishes washed up, dried and put away whilst he was in cleaning-up mode. Arkwright, full of anger, told the lad that he was not a person to be meddled with. (Sadly, Arkwright's classes in English had not been extended to taking in the rule that you do not end a sentence with a preposition).

The cameraman attended to his duties – and to make sure there was to be no shirking, Arkwright put his sheep dog in the kitchen to watch over the photographer. The sheep dog had an uncanny knowledge of the English language and could be relied upon to ensure that the photographer did not leave the kitchen until his master's wishes had been fulfilled.

Only when all had been accomplished did the dog wag his tail, jump up at the photographer and perform a not unnatural act (well, not unnatural for a dog) against his leg. Perhaps it was because the dog was called Oliver, and the photographer called Roland, that a strange psychic bond seemed to exist between the two of them – at least, so far as Oliver was concerned.

'Now, Mr Broughton,' Seth began. 'What do you know about this whole affair?'

Arkwright had to confess that the events of the day had come upon him as something of a bolt out of the blue. 'Me and Doris,' he began, 'have always been a happy couple. I've never had to remind her of my congenital rights and, when of an evening I've felt the old man stirring, she's never once said that she had a rotten headache. Not that I've ever forced meself upon her,' he was quick to add. But as to when she'd ever had it away with Old Tom was quite beyond him. 'I allus kept her well served. Perhaps it happened before we were wed – I can't see that Old Tom was up to it much after then. We'd gotten engaged when we were thirty apiece and by that time Old Tom was sixty – and that's over thirty years ago.'

The reporter reminded Arkwright that Charlie Chaplin was still fathering children when he was over eighty. All Arkwright could say to that was, 'Lucky bugger!'

Seth Womersley could see large pound signs before his eyes. Here was a story he could sell to the national press which might lead, who knows, to a job for him with one of the London papers. The search was on to find Doris – and Seth wanted to be the first to find her. Not that Seth let Arkwright in on that secret.

Arkwright did consider taking himself off to the Cat and Fiddle but put the notion out of his head. Too many prying folk down there, he thought to himself. But then, the need for some company grew on him and, who knows, somebody might mention to him, in passing, that they'd seen Doris thereabouts. It was a chance and a price Arkwright was prepared to take.

The village church clock struck eight as Arkwright walked into the pub. Mercifully, the regulars had all got their pints in so there was no first round for him to stand. He joined Ben Driglington who was standing in his usual place at the end of the bar as he chatted up *mine host*, Jessie Tasker.

'I see you're in the money, Arkwright,' Ben said, 'but let me buy you a drink to celebrate.' He also offered one to Jessie who, he noticed, didn't give herself a drink but put its cost in a beer glass by the till.

'What's Doris going to do with all the money?' Ben asked.

'To be honest,' Arkwright replied dishonestly, 'she's not made any plans yet. We've discussed a few ideas but it's all come as a bit of a shock to us both, so I suggested to her that she went away for a few days til its all old news. I'm going to join her later this week after I've had chance to get fixed up with someone to look after my beasts and hens whilst I'll be away.'

'I'll not ask you about Doris and Old Tom's baby,' Jessie began, 'but . . .'

'Well don't ask then,' Arkwright interrupted very tartly. 'Nothing rum's been afoot between my Doris and Old Tom Bones, so you can all stop thinking summat's been up between them. We don't know why Old Tom's done what he's done, but we'll find out right enough, and that'll put a stop to all the wagging tongues.'

Ben Driglington intervened to pour oil on troubled waters. 'Now then, Arkwright,' he said, 'you mustn't take on so. It's only natural that folk are curious – it's come as a bit of a shock to all of us. None of us had any idea that Old Tom Bones had so much brass, and we all know, really, that nothing ever went on between him and your Doris. But people are going to talk and there's nothing you can do about it. You've got friends down here at the pub, and we're not going to put up with people who want to gossip about you and Doris.'

By now the other regulars had joined Arkwright and Ben Driglington at the bar. 'That's right,' they all said, almost in unison. And it was agreed between them that none of them would mention again the subject of Doris and her inheritance, and Old Tom Bones' child.

Arkwright expressed his gratitude for the show of mutual solidarity and stood them all a drink. He supped up and declined the offer of another jar of ale from Ben Driglington.

As soon as he was out of the pub, Arkwright, Doris, her inheritance and Old Tom's child became the sole topic of conversation. Arkwright knew it would be so. It would be some time before he took another trip to the Cat and Fiddle.

Chapter 4

The Private Drawer

Doris Broughton was holed up somewhere in England, but quite where that was, her husband knew not.

Arkwright had been fearful of phoning round his family and friends because he was acutely embarrassed at having to own up to being deserted by his wife. It was not a matter to be shouted from the roof top – even if he knew that not a few of his male friends wished that their wives would conveniently disappear. Notwithstanding her faults – and Arkwright could list few – he was genuinely fond of Doris.

But as the news that Doris was missing was now very much in the public domain, Arkwright could start on the long list of phone calls he thought he ought to make. Not that there was too much need for such activity on his part, as everybody seemed to be phoning him. 'It's better that the calls should be on their phone bills than mine,' he muttered every time he had to answer the phone.

Amongst the earliest of the telephone calls he received was one from Ethel Ollerenshaw – Doris' sister. Now Ethel and Arkwright had never hit it off. He had formed the opinion that she was none too bright when he had once been talking to her about Sherlock Holmes and Ethel thought he was talking about a municipal dwelling for the elderly and incontinent.

Ethel might well have had a gaping hole in her head between her ears, but that was more than compensated for by her sharp tongue and substantial lungs. Ethel was one of those who, when she phoned, never let you get a word in edgeways. And if, by mischance on her part, she ever suffered a momentary lack of concentration and a pause occurred which allowed you to start speaking, then her voice would rise several decibels above yours and she would finish off your sentence as she thought fit, and then return speedily to what she had been addressing at you.

After several years of this treatment from Ethel, Arkwright had hit upon the expedient device of depositing the telephone receiver on the table, returning to it from time to time to say 'Yes' or 'No' before quietly putting it back down on the table again. Once, he had busied himself with the crossword during one such call and had become so wrapped up in it that he had forgotten totally that Ethel was on the phone to him. When the recollection came back to him he broke out into a cold sweat and dashed back to the recumbent phone only to find that the line was dead. Ethel was a person one ignored at one's peril.

Arkwright thought that his day of Armageddon had arrived and retribution for his sin would surely be visited upon him. But no such day of grand reckoning came. Thereafter, whenever Ethel phoned he just put the receiver down and continued to engage himself in whatever he had been occupied with before the phone had rung. And, seemingly, Ethel was never any the wiser.

But today was different. Doris was missing and Arkwright felt he was obliged to listen to the call.

'Where's Doris?' snapped Ethel with such ferocity that Arkwright thought he was going to suffer a perforated ear drum.

Before he could utter a word, Ethel had launched into a diatribe the like of which Arkwright had never heard before. He reflected that he'd probably have heard more moderate language had he eavesdropped on the lurid conversations of the fisherwomen of Whitby.

'I've always said the marriage wouldn't last,' Ethel bellowed – conveniently forgetting the marriage had already endured over thirty years. Ethel was long on rhetoric, but short on logic.

When the phone call had begun, Arkwright had thought Ethel might have had some intelligence as to where his beloved Doris was but, as he gathered his senses, he knew instinctively that Doris was too bright ever to seek refuge with her sister or even to confide a private thought in her.

Over the years, Arkwright had endured too many of these one-sided phonecalls from his sister-in-law, and he was in no mood for one today. Pulling himself to his full height, he raised his voice over that of Ethel's and told her she would do better to keep her mouth shut and be thought a fool, than open it and prove it. When he had finished, he slammed the phone down. It came as no surprise to Arkwright that Ethel never phoned him again. Years afterwards, when Arkwright and Doris had been reconciled, Arkwright considered that that phone call had been one of the more positive aspects coming out of what he called 'The Doris Incident.'

But where was Doris?

The ghost of Old Tom Bones continued to haunt Arkwright and the whole village. Indeed, the interest of the whole Dale had been aroused by the goings-on. Arkwright and Doris had always been considered pillars of their local community. That Doris had once 'had it away' with Old Tom Bones was beyond everybody's comprehension. Even in his finer days, Old Tom Bones had never been considered – in modern day parlance – Mr Macho Man or even Mr Romeo. His perpetual sniffle and adenoidal problems were grounds in themselves to preclude any romantic attachment with him. But Old Tom Bones had left Doris his very considerable estate. You don't get owt for nowt, the Dales folk were quick to point out – and some could not help but believe that, no matter what the size of the estate, it was cheap for the price of a frolic with Old Tom Bones now no longer of the parish.

But Doris was missing and, as they say, 'There's no smoke without fire.'

Now as it happened, Arkwright remembered that Doris had always kept in touch with Betty Entwistle, an old school chum. Arkwright had last met Betty at his wedding but she had moved to London many years ago and their contact over the years had diminished to the exchange of Christmas cards with a brief letter stuffed inside it. Arkwright knew that Doris would have left the Dale and gone somewhere where she could be assured of anonymity. London would afford that to Doris.

Arkwright and Doris had always respected each other's privacy and he would not normally have considered looking through the contents of her dressing table drawer. These were not, though, normal circumstances, and he felt justified in trespassing on the privacy of Doris' special drawer. There, he found Betty's address.

So it was, as the Dales were bathed in sunshine, Arkwright found himself on a train London bound.

Chapter 5

Doris in London

Like so many young people setting out in life, Doris had not always been an exemplar of fiscal rectitude in the management of her bank account. On more than one occasion in her heady youthful days she had been summoned to meet with her Bank Manager to discuss measures to 'regularise' her account. But those days were now well behind her and she was, as they say in banking parlance, now always 'in funds'.

It had been something of a shock, therefore, for Doris to find herself receiving an early morning call from Mr Grimsdyke, her bank manager, asking her to call in on him that very morning. The surprise turned almost to fear when he adamantly refused to tell her over the phone the nature of the business he wished to conduct with her – save to say that it was urgent – *very urgent*.

Fortunately for Doris, her husband was out of the house when the call came through. Had he been aware that the Dale's premier financial institution was peremptorily summoning his wife to its hallowed portals . . . well, Doris could only imagine the 'to-do' he would have made of it and the interminable interrogation to which he would have subjected her. But she had been spared that drama.

Doris managed to slip out of the house before Arkwright had got back from feeding the chickens. She made her way to the bank and was promptly ushered into the presence of Mr Grimsdyke.

Apart from Mr Grimsdyke, Doris wondered whether anybody else wore pinstripe trousers and wing collars in the countryside. His distinctive attire certainly set him apart from the rest of the

Dale's folk and, with his lugubrious countenance, he was no doubt often confused with the village undertaker by those who did not know who he was.

Once inside the office, Doris was offered the most comfortable chair on which to park herself. Tea and biscuits were brought in and Mr Grimsdyke almost grovelled at her feet as the custard creams were extended by him in her direction. This was not quite the treatment Doris had ever experienced in the past from the bank manager, even though her account had always been in funds for forty years and more. So taken aback was Doris by this treatment of her that her mind began to entertain hitherto unimaginable ideas. 'Does he fancy me? Is he going to make a pass at me?' Certainly, so far as she was aware, she had never given him any expectations in the direction – but with bank managers you never knew what they were thinking. Making music with Mr Grimsdyke was not a prospect she had ever contemplated, and the notion that he might be wanting to play his swan song with her was not one which immediately commended itself to her.

'Now it's like this,' Mr Grimsdyke began. 'As you are perhaps aware, I am the executor of the Last Will and Testament of the late Mr Thomas Bones. He came to see me a few months ago about the disposition of his estate, which amounts to a very considerable sum of money. Indeed, it turns out to be in the region of three million pounds. In his discussions with me he took me into his confidence and, against an absolute assurance on my part that no details would be made public until after his death, he told me a tale I found hard to believe.

'Now what occurred in the past between you and Mr Bones – two consenting adults – is of no concern to me as a bank manager and, whilst I was mightily astounded to hear the words which passed from his lips, it was not within my province then – or now – to express any personal opinion. What Mr Bones told me was that you had borne him a child at some time in the past and he felt that, on his death, it was time for him to acknowledge that fact and to recompense you. Accordingly, I have to tell you that Mr Bones has left you his entire estate.'

Doris was flabbergasted. The tale she had been told was like her worst dream having come true. She sat in the chair – dumbstruck.

'It's not as it seems,' was all she could say to Mr Grimsdyke. 'There are matters which need to get sorted out and I'm not in a position to discuss these with you at this precise moment in time.'

Although Mr Grimsdyke could well understand the nature and extent of the shock he had just inflicted on Doris Broughton, he asked her gently to try and be plain with him, and to tell him what she could of the matter. She eventually agreed, and told him a story which he found difficult to believe. Having heard the facts of the case, he realised that she clearly needed time to collect her thoughts, assemble her arguments and organise her defence before she had to confront her husband with the hidden truth which he had just been privileged to hear. He was not, though, about to entangle himself in a domestic dispute of this nature.

As a devout chapel man, he deplored the seemingly wayward life Doris had once led. To him, the money which was about to come her way was tainted money – dirty money. Money he certainly couldn't ever touch – leastwise, not in a personal capacity. But it was not for him to judge the morals of others and to pronounce upon them. However . . . as a bank manager he had responsibilities to his bank which transcended his own moral values. Doris would need help and advice on how to invest her new-found wealth. Morally, he had a responsibility to her in that respect – and, not least of all, he needed no reminding of the revenues his bank would earn from his stewardship of this new-found wealth. 'God moves in a mysterious way,' he thought to himself as he suddenly saw the profitability of his own branch of the bank moving upwards.

Doris stood up to go. She told Mr Grimsdyke that she would need a little time and space to consider her position and that she would be in touch with him again, shortly.

As Doris briskly walked back home she considered her alternatives. She could face Arkwright now – but she knew he was inclined to immoderate verbal statements in his immediate reactions to startling news, and what was called for now was calm deliberation. Her second thought was to disappear for a few days and make certain arrangements before returning to the Dale to set matters straight with Arkwright and the wagging tongues of the village.

Setting the record straight from afar was, without doubt, the most preferable course for her to take. In due course, she knew Arkwright would understand her sudden disappearance and forgive her the brief note she would leave him which left so much unexplained.

It was several hours later that a surprised Betty Entwistle found her old school friend standing outside the front door of her home in London.

Chapter 6

Arkwright finds Doris

Arkwright had once been on a day trip to Ripon but what with all that traffic in the market place – and the noise – he was glad when he was back in his sleepy village. Against such a background, he was therefore totally unprepared for London.

The train journey to the capital was a geography lesson come alive for Arkwright. Places which he had previously only known as big dots on a map flashed before his eyes – York, Doncaster, Peterborough and, not least of all, Welwyn Garden City, from whence came his daily Welgar Shredded Wheats.

As the train approached London, a man sitting opposite Arkwright pointed out to his son the place where Arsenal played football. But as a Leeds United supporter, Arkwright averted his gaze from the window at the very mention of the name of Arsenal.

Arkwright hadn't ever actually seen a proper game of football played and he knew little – indeed, nothing – about the sport. Whilst he had occasionally heard commentaries of matches on his faithful wireless set they had never excited him sufficiently enough so that he had gone out and bought himself a telly so he could see what really happened at a proper football match.

During the Saturday evenings he spent at the Cat and Fiddle, Arkwright had often heard the name 'Arsenal' mentioned. What he'd heard was not good. Seemingly, Arsenal were, at best, lucky and, at worst, cheats – and they frequently robbed Leeds United whenever they played a match together. With Arkwright's natural and instinctive dislike of southerners it was inevitable that he had become a supporter of Leeds United and had a deep-rooted hatred of Arsenal.

When the train pulled into Kings Cross Station, Arkwright took his small case down from the luggage rack and waited by the door for the train to stop. Not surprisingly for one who found Ripon to be confusing, London was going to present him with problems. It would be nearer the mark to say that Arkwright was totally bewildered and not a little terrified by his new surroundings. He knew that Betty Entwistle lived in Chiswick and he had rather assumed that it would be but a short walk down the road from the station. He was very much mistaken.

In no time at all he was completely lost. He didn't know where he was or how he'd got there. It therefore came as something of a relief when he espied a callow youth standing idly on a street corner. Arkwright gave him a traditionally friendly north country greeting and the youth asked if he was 'looking for business.' It was only the approaching presence of a policeman which spared Arkwright from having his innocence exposed.

The policeman was helpful. He walked Arkwright back to Kings Cross Station, helped him to buy his underground ticket and wrote down where and when he had to change stations and lines on the tube to get to Chiswick. 'By gum, lad,' Arkwright told the policeman, 'we've got nowt like this where I come from.' He thought nothing of it when the constable readily accepted the fiver he had offered as recompense for his time and assistance.

By now it was early evening and Arkwright thought it would be inconsiderate of him to arrive unexpectedly on Betty's doorstep at that hour. After all, if Doris were with her they would probably want to be alone on their first nights together after so many years of absence to talk about the 'good old days' and the reason for her sudden appearance. In any event, making up a third bed unexpectedly might have presented Betty with a problem. He decided to await the morning before presenting himself on the threshold of Betty's door.

It didn't take Arkwright long to find a bed and breakfast establishment which looked clean and welcoming. The landlady was called Maggie. Arkwright had once known a Maggie in his village. She had been a rebellious young girl who, against the wishes of her parents, had run off and married a soldier. The rebellious streak she had shown against her parents soon manifested itself in her marital military life where she kicked three colonels, two majors, four captains and one Mills bomb. But this Maggie was different – not least of all because she was still alive.

Arkwright had seen a McDonald's on his way to his bed and breakfast accommodation. He'd never been to a McDonald's before but the young folk in his village seemed to speak highly of them. He told Maggie of his proposed evening eating arrangements – but she would have nothing of them. Recognising that he was in a different world here in London, she insisted that he share her evening meal with her. It was only after Arkwright insisted, and she had agreed, that his share of the meal be put on his bill that he accepted the hospitality being offered.

Perhaps it was the wine which loosened Arkwright's tongue but by the end of the meal he had told all to Maggie.

'If I'd gone into our bedroom and seen Doris and Old Tom Bones together,' he told Maggie, 'I'd have been surprised.'

'No!' said Maggie. 'If you'd seen them together in bed you'd have been astounded – Doris is the one who'd have been surprised. But do you think that ever really happened? From what you've told me, both you and Doris have been happily married for so many years. I can't believe this ever happened in your married life together. And if it happened before then, then it's best forgotten. Remember, she chose you to be married to, and not Tom Bones.'

From her brief acquaintanceship with Arkwright she just knew that he could never ever have sown any wild oats. Any suggestion that Doris might have been unfaithful to him as an act of revenge would, therefore, be a totally inappropriate idea for her even to suggest to Arkwright.

'Remember what you are now. Remember all that you have had in your life together,' Maggie said. 'In my case, marriage wasn't a word – it was a sentence; but for you and Doris it's been something better. See Doris tomorrow. Be quiet and hear out what she's got to say.'

Looking at the crucifix hanging on her dining room wall, Maggie said, 'And now abideth these three – Faith, Hope and Charity, and the greatest of these is Charity. Show charity towards Doris – show love towards Doris, for love conquers all.' With that she got up from the table, and planted a soft kiss on Arkwright's balding head. Arkwright felt close to tears.

No one was less aware of the Scriptures than Arkwright. Whilst nobody would ever believe that Arkwright had committed adultery – let alone enjoyed sex before marriage – he was aware that he had fallen short of righteousness in almost every aspect of his life. After all, he would have happily left the dishes for Doris to clear up after she had come home. 'Let him without sin cast the first stone' came to Arkwright's mind. Arkwright knew, deep down, that when the final trump sounded he would be found wanting. But he was not going to tell Doris of the several indiscretions which could be laid at his door.

Maggie was not only a good cook but she was something of a philosopher. She might not be Brain of Britain but you did not need to be that to talk common sense. Arkwright went to bed that night a wiser man.

He rose early the following morning and, like the condemned man, ate a hearty breakfast. Half an hour later he was standing on the doorstep of 103 Chiswick High Road ringing the doorbell.

It was Doris who answered the door.

Chapter 7

Facing the Truth

When the doorbell rang, Betty Entwistle was in the middle of her morning ablutions. Doris Broughton had already showered and dressed – and so it was she who went to answer the door.

The sight of her husband standing on the doorstep came as a profound shock to Doris. It was sufficient for her to go weak at the knees and totter unsteadily on her feet. Arkwright, seeing Doris swaying in front of him, moved forward to catch her. 'Nay, lass,' he said, 'we can work all this out together.'

Doris led Arkwright into the lounge. An embarrassed silence followed them. Doris sat on the settee and Arkwright in one of the two easy chairs. The embarrassed silence hung in the air.

It was Arkwright who spoke first. 'Now then,' he said, 'what's all this about? Where's this child of yours?'

Doris studied the floor. 'None of this should ever have happened. Old Tom Bones is trying to get back at me from beyond the grave because I thwarted him.

'Years ago, well before we were even walking out together, he asked me to wed him and I refused – even though I did hold a certain affection for him. One night when I was walking home from a Women's Institute meeting he suddenly appeared in front of me out of nowhere and said he needed to talk to me right urgently.'

Before Doris could continue, Betty Entwistle poked her head round the door of the lounge to see who it was Doris had let into her house.

'Why, Arkwright!' she fair exclaimed, 'this is a surprise!'

28

Arkwright stood up to shake hands with her but Betty made to give him a kiss on both cheeks totally ignoring his outstretched hand – which somewhat flummoxed him. It wasn't quite the way people greeted each other in the Dales but Arkwright remembered he was now in London where perhaps things were done a bit differently. Probably, he thought, London being that bit nearer to France foreign ways had crept into their habits.

To be kissed on one cheek by Betty Entwistle was bad enough – but to be kissed on both was like being smacked across the face by a wet kipper. Arkwright had suffered the double disappointment of being too young to be soldier in the First World War and too old for the battlefield in the Second. But he stood his ground like the trooper he'd never been and, stoically facing up to the unexpected onslaught against his person, bravely puckered up his lips advancing them towards Betty's fast approaching cheeks.

Betty was mindful of the fact that Doris and Arkwright would want to be alone. Now that she had ascertained who the caller had been at her front door she could return to the task of preparing herself for the eight o'clock train to the City where she worked. However, notwithstanding the fact that it was still so early in the morning she felt obliged to be a good hostess by offering her guests a glass of sherry. Despite the early hour for an alcoholic beverage, Arkwright gratefully accepted, believing it would fortify him for what lay ahead.

Pouring out two generous measures, Betty said, 'I keep this bottle only for my best friends.'

Arkwright, having taken a sip, said that he didn't blame her. Betty took the remark to be a compliment and left the room bathed in her own gleam of pride.

'Well,' said Arkwright. 'What was it that was so urgent that Old Tom Bones had to tell you.'

Doris bit her lip hard to stop it from trembling, but she knew she could not delay continuing with her story.

'Way back in the past,' Doris said, 'Old Tom Bones tried to seduce me. I'd let him kiss me on the lips but when he tried to go a bit further I slapped his face. I can tell you that he was mightily surprised, and he told me that little Bessie Sidebottom had been much more receptive to his advances.

29

'I asked him what he meant by that, and he said she'd let him go all the way. Well, I told him that his luck had changed if he thought he was going to do unto me what he'd done unto her. He mumbled what sounded like an apology and ran off as though the Devil was chasing him.

'After that we both kept out of each other's way – until that night when he suddenly appeared in front of me from out of nowhere.'

'By gum,' said Arkwright, 'I'd heard rumours that he was into animal husbandry until the RSPCA threatened to prosecute him, but I'd never thought of him doing it with any of the lasses in the village.' Arkwright reflected momentarily on what he had just been told. He could only assume that little Bessie Sidebottom, who was so ugly when she was born that the midwife had slapped her mother's face, had thought it best to seize any opportunity for intimacy for fear that Opportunity would not visit her again.

Some of the village had always said that little Bessie Sidebottom was weak in the head. But feeble or not, she'd clearly known it was better to let the grass grow under her back than under her feet.

Doris resumed her tale of woe. 'You'll remember the time when little Bessie mistook a bulge for a curve and left the village all of a sudden to look after a dying aunt – well, Old Tom Bones told me that night that little Bessie had actually gone off to have his baby at his aunt's house somewhere in Somerset. Shortly after the baby was born, little Bessie returned to the village keeping the secret to herself. She never enquired after the baby and, seemingly, neither did Old Tom Bones and the aunt was left to raise the child on her own.

'Six months after the baby was born, Old Tom Bones got a letter from his aunt saying the baby had died – and he thought that was the end of the matter. But it wasn't, because it appears the aunt put the baby away in an orphanage.

'About ten years ago Old Tom Bones received a letter from the social services saying that his son wanted to get in touch with him. The news came something as a shock because he'd believed for years that his son was dead. Perhaps it was because of the shame of it, or because of his guilty conscience, but he told me he couldn't bring himself to allow his son to meet him.

'It was after he'd got that letter that Old Tom Bones stopped me that night. He said that unless I agreed to help him he would tell everybody that the baby was mine. I couldn't believe what he was saying.'

Doris began to cry. Arkwright didn't know what to do. He wasn't a man of great education and, whilst he could help a cow in distress, he wasn't up to much when it came to handling human emotions. He rose from his chair and went to sit beside Doris on the settee. He held her hand and stroked it gently.

'What was it Old Tom Bones wanted you to do?' Arkwright asked.

'He said he wanted me to agree to meet the boy on his behalf and tell him that his father had lost his faculties and that I was his mother. He said he couldn't bear it if the lad found out that little Bessie Sidebottom was the mother, what with her not being all there in the head.

'I told him it was out of the question for me to deceive his son in that way, and that it would be cruel to little Bessie. He told me that little Bessie need never know and, in any event, what with her being feeble in the head, she wouldn't understand what was happening. I told him straight that what he was doing was nothing short of blackmail, and that I'd have nothing to do with his plan.

'We stood and argued for some time and a sad look came over his face. He said I'd understand one day why he was asking me to do him that favour, but he wouldn't say any more. In the end he said he'd get someone to write to the authorities. The subject was never mentioned again and I thought that was that until I got a phone call to go and see Mr Grimsdyke at the bank.

'I told Mr Grimsdyke what I've told you and he said he couldn't do anything about the Will being published the next day. He told me to go home and talk to you about it all, but I just couldn't do it. I got all confused and wanted to get away before the village tongues started wagging and people pointed fingers at me. I'm sorry that I left you to face it all on your own, but I'm right glad that you came and found me.

'I did tell Mr Grimsdyke that I wouldn't accept the money and he promised to speak to Old Tom Bones' solicitor to see if any papers could be found amongst Old Tom's possessions which might clear the matter up.

'I asked him what was to be done about little Bessie Sidebottom and he said he'd have to see what any documents he could find might say before he could go and talk to her. Until it's all sorted out, I just can't go back to the Dale.'

Arkwright put his arm round his beloved Doris. 'Don't fret yourself, love,' he said. 'It'll all work out right in the end. At least I now know the truth of the matter.'

Arkwright told Doris that she should stay with Betty whilst he went back home to see Mr Grimsdyke to find out if he had been able to unearth any facts about the boy.

That afternoon, Arkwright was back at Kings Cross Station. But the news he was going to receive from Mr Grimsdyke when he got back to the Dale was going to give him a nasty shock.

Chapter 8

Arkwright in Turmoil

On his arrival back in the village, Arkwright was met by Seth
Womersley of the *Gazette* who, it transpired, had spent the greater
part of the past couple of days nosing around the village asking
questions.

This was Seth's first real piece of investigative journalism and,
thus far, it was going badly. No one in the village to whom he had
spoken knew – or was prepared to admit to knowing – where Doris
had gone. And everybody had expressed equal surprise when it
looked as though Arkwright had also gone missing. His cows that
morning had gone unmilked and would have remained so but for
Walter Wainright who had noticed their distress.

Most of the villagers were standing foursquare behind Doris and
Arkwright. Folk found the idea of an affair between Doris and Old
Tom Bones both bewildering and bizarre, but they were confident
that explanations would soon be forthcoming which would clear up
the whole sordid business – after which the village would return to
its former tranquil life.

But not all of the villagers were of that mind. There were those
who relished nothing more than a good gossip – and the murkier it
was, the better. Alice Oglethorpe was the leader of that crusading
band.

Mrs Oglethorpe, having been the late Old Tom Bones' 'woman
what does' for upwards of twenty years had held very considerable
expectations that Old Tom would remember her in his Will. She
had always reckoned that attending to his soiled pants and hankies

– and generally cleaning up after an untrained bachelor – would ultimately be rewarded by more than the £1.50 per hour she had been recompensed with for her domestic services during the past two decades. But this had not come about – and now Doris Broughton was going to inherit all Old Tom Bones' estate because of some hanky-panky between them in the past. In the eyes of Mrs Oglethorpe this fell well short of natural justice and she saw it as her bounden duty to redress the balance of opinion in the village, which was currently well in favour of the Broughtons. For those who had ears to hear, Alice Oglethorpe would vent her spleen and seek to darken the name of Doris Broughton. Seth Womersley was one who had ears to hear.

Seth considered the idea of confronting Arkwright with the facts he had gleaned from Mrs Oglethorpe but, in the end, refrained from doing so. He needed more solid evidence that the rantings of a woman scorned, before a second bombshell was dropped on the village. Seth therefore contented himself with asking Arkwright if he had any news of Mrs Broughton.

'I've nowt to say, lad,' Arkwright responded firmly. And with that he disappeared indoors to phone Mr Grimsdyke.

Half an hour later, Arkwright set off for the bank. Seth Womersley followed – but at a discrete distance.

Arkwright and Mr Grimsdyke exchanged perfunctory handshakes. Arkwright did wonder what the reaction of the bank manager would have been had he greeted him with a kiss on both cheeks – but matters were too serious for such frivolous conjecture.

'I've got the birth certificate of the boy,' Mr Grimsdyke began, 'which has been found amongst the papers of the late Mr Bones. It's the birth certificate of James Arkwright Bones. The name of the mother is given as Doris Ollerenshaw – that's your wife's maiden name isn't it?'

Blood drained from Arkwright's face. His mind was in a turmoil. 'It just can't be true,' he said to Mr Grimsdyke. Arkwright couldn't believe that all Doris had told him earlier that day had been a pack of lies. He took the birth certificate in his hands so that he could see with his own eyes what was written on it. There it was in black and white. There was no disputing it – James *Arkwright* Bones whose mother was his wife and whose father he was not.

'No. No. No,' Arkwright kept repeating to Mr Grimsdyke. 'There must be more papers than this birth certificate about the lad and how Old Tom Bones had come to put Doris' name down as the mother without her consent. No. I don't believe it. What Doris told me today was the truth. Old Tom Bones is just trying to get even with her just because she wouldn't wed him those long years ago.'

'I know it's hard to accept,' Mr Grimsdyke said, 'but Old Tom is given as the father and Mrs Broughton is clearly stated as being the mother. I just don't see how it can be otherwise. I can ask Mr Driglington to see if he can uncover any other papers which might give us some more information, but I can't see what else he will find to show the facts aren't as they are stated on this birth certificate.'

Arkwright asked Mr Grimsdyke to get Ben Driglington to search again through all of Old Tom's papers. 'I can't tell you why right now, but I know for a fact that Doris isn't the mother of this child,' he told the bank manager.

It was a tired Arkwright Broughton who left the bank that afternoon. And he wasn't best pleased when Seth Womersley began to pester him again as he walked back home.

'I'll not tell thee again,' Arkwright told Seth. 'I've nowt to say and if you keep on pestering me I'll have to police after you.'

Remembering that discretion was the better part of valour, Seth decided to give Arkwright Broughton a wide berth – at least for the time being.

Chapter 9

Little Bessie Sidebottom

Little Bessie Sidebottom stood well over six-foot tall. She had acquired the sobriquet 'little' well before she had started infant school. Not having much else going for her at the time she enjoyed her nickname.

It must have been when she was about eleven years old that she began to take notice of the opposite sex. Being a tall and well-developed child it was easy for her to be taken as being much older. Sadly, though, her brain worked none too fast.

Little Bessie was only called 'Daft Bessie' once. Those who stood by watching her lay into the caller of that name learnt their lesson with him – and those who were not there listened in awe as the tale was told of how, with a single blow, she had felled Freddie Sheepshanks.

It wouldn't be quite true to say that little Bessie didn't prosper at school. For a silver sixpence, paid in advance, she would conduct her own brand of extracurricular biology lessons behind the bicycle sheds. In his time at the school, Arkwright Broughton had spent more than a bob or two having his education broadened by little Bessie.

It was inevitable that, one day, her activities would be discovered. Her parents had become quite alarmed at the regular amounts little Bessie was depositing in her Post Office Savings Account. They approached the school and it was agreed that her Form Mistress, Dolly Lumby, would keep a special eye on her. The truth of what was happening emerged at the midday break when Miss Lumby caught little Bessie 'playing at schools'. When Miss Lumby asked about the pile of sixpenny pieces stacked neatly on the wall, little Bessie had replied with words to the effect that hers was a fee-paying school.

The following day little Bessie announced to her parents that the vicar had taken the morning assembly and told them about the dangers of sex. As he had wiped his spectacles he had told them that sex would make them go blind. Thereafter, whenever little Bessie saw anybody wearing glasses she would give them a rather disconcerting snort and snigger.

Although little Bessie was not gifted academically, she had some sense of logic. On being asked by a visiting School Inspector what logarithms were, she had suggested they were a form of wooden dance music. And when she had been asked to explain what the word 'straight' meant, she had replied 'without water'. But such wisdom did not advance little Bessie far at school, and by the time it came for her to leave the sacred groves of academe she was without any qualifications.

Had little Bessie been living in Leeds or Bradford she would have ended up at the local mill. But there were no mills in Widdledale. Little Bessie was both unemployed and unemployable.

Days passed into weeks, weeks into months and months into years without little Bessie having remunerated employment. And then an opportunity arose for her.

For some weeks, Arkwright Broughton had been having trouble 'down below'. His waterworks were in need of some repair and he required an able-bodied person to help out on the farm to do the heavy work whilst he was in the district hospital being attended to. What with her bad back, such work could not be left to Doris. Little Bessie may not have been Arkwright's first choice for the vacancy on his farm but she was the village's only unemployment statistic.

On his return from hospital, Arkwright was on light duties only, so little Bessie stayed on at the farm, and Arkwright was much surprised at the work little Bessie had done during his absence and Doris couldn't speak too highly of her. Indeed, she had made herself so indispensable that both Doris and Arkwright eventually decided that they should permanently employ her.

Arkwright was always an early riser but Doris preferred to stay abed until well after the cock had crowed. It was Arkwright's normal practice to have his Welgar Shredded Wheats and then go to feed his chickens. After that he milked the cows and then returned to the farmhouse. Doris would still be in bed so he would take her a full breakfast of fried bacon, eggs, and, if they were available from his fields, mushrooms. On special occasions such as their wedding

Arkwright sees Tom Bones and Bessie Sidebottom in the hayloft

anniversary he would have gathered a bunch of wild flowers from the hedgerows and placed them in a vase on her tray. Such things meant much to Doris and she counted her blessings at having married such a man as Arkwright.

It would be about an hour after her breakfast that Doris would eventually emerge. She would carry her tray downstairs and clear up the mess Arkwright had left in the kitchen. By then, Arkwright would be back out on the farm attending to the day's tasks.

On one such day, Arkwright had occasion to visit the hayloft. There, before him, lay Old Tom Bones and little Bessie with their clothes in considerable disarray. He watched the two of them at it for a while and memories of his spent sixpenny pieces came flooding back to him. Little Bessie was playing 'teacher' again – but at a more advanced level than when he was a learner at her school. Arkwright crept away unobserved. But the excitement of the moment he had unwittingly observed remained with him. He wondered how many times in the past little Bessie and Old Tom Bones had enjoyed a frolic in his barn during little Bessie's working hours. And he couldn't help but wonder whether Old Tom Bones was the only recipient of little Bessie's favours on his premises.

Arkwright said nothing to Old Tom Bones or to little Bessie about what he had witnessed that morning. Nor did he tell Doris.

When Arkwright returned to the house for lunch he looked at Doris in a new light. There she was solid, dependable, the best housewife in the Dale – and barren.

Chapter 10

The Diaries

Alice Oglethorpe had always known that Old Tom Bones had taken a shine to Doris Broughton.

Although she wasn't a resident of the village at the time Doris and Old Tom had briefly been seen together in public, talk of it had been rekindled since the Last Will and Testament of Old Tom had become public knowledge. But the village folk knew that the relationship between them had only been a temporary liaison and that it had finished well before she and Arkwright started stepping out together.

The village folk also knew full well that both at the time of her dalliance with Old Tom, and since then, Doris had never been out of the village for a single day – that is, apart from her trip to America with Arkwright and her solitary day's outing to Bridlington with the Mothers' Union. Had she ever known Old Tom in the biblical sense then the effects of such knowledge would have been so evident that it could not have escaped the attention of the entire village. Certainly, Doris could never have had Old Tom's child.

What the villagers did not also know was that Doris was barren. Doris knew, therefore, beyond peradventure that she could not have had Old Tom's baby – let alone that of anybody else. Whilst she had on occasions seen a star in the east as she gazed out of the window of a night, it had never made her womb leap.

It had always been something of a surprise in the village that the Broughtons had never had any children. Doris was known as 'Aunty Doris' to so many of the village children and she had led the church cub pack until advanced years made it sensible that she should hang up her woggle and allow a younger and more energetic person take over from her. If further evidence of Doris' love for children were needed, merely to look on her face at a church christening was sufficient announcement that Doris had a real love of children.

The general conclusion had been reached in the village that the absence of the patter of tiny feet in the Broughton household must be due to some deficiency on the part of Arkwright. Not that any dared to make that suggestion in his presence.

Arkwright also knew that Doris was barren and it confused him not a little that Old Tom Bones was saying from beyond the grave that she had born him a son. But the evidence was there in the form of a birth certificate. Perhaps she hadn't always been as barren as they had both supposed and perhaps she had once had a fling with Old Tom Bones which had caught them both out. Not being a medical man, Arkwright just didn't know now what to believe. All Arkwright did know was that it was not through any lack of energy and effort on his part that he had no heir – not that he'd ever had himself tested in that department.

Not wishing to malign 'women what do' it could be said with some certainty that, in the exercise of their domestic duties, they do come across papers and letters in the households they clean. And that whilst they never disclose the information that they have come by *accidentally*, the knowledge always stays with them. Such was the case of Alice Oglethorpe who once chanced to read some of the diaries of Old Tom Bones when she was tidying up his desk.

The diaries revealed Old Tom's abiding love of Doris and told in intimate detail all of the meetings they'd had together. They also told of Old Tom's goings-on with little Bessie Sidebottom and, not least of all, of what little Bessie had once told him about Arkwright. No less interesting was Old Tom's account of what happened when he had confronted Doris Broughton the evening he had asked for her help.

When Alice Oglethorpe had read in the *Gazette* of Old Tom Bones' Last Will and Testament she had gone round immediately to his house and removed the diaries. She was later to say that she took them so that they did not fall into unscrupulous hands and that

41

it was her intention to burn them because of the harm which would result if the contents became public knowledge.

And now, Alice Oglethorpe was meeting with Seth Womersley in her front parlour.

Seth had already heard what Mrs Oglethorpe proclaimed to all in the village who had ears to hear. He had been intrigued by what he had heard and she accepted with some speed his suggestion that he come to visit her at her cottage where it would be more private and where she could talk more freely.

'I can prove what I've already told you,' she said to Seth, 'but I think I should be recompensed. If I went to the *News of the World* with my story I could become a rich woman. Life hasn't been easy for me since my husband died.'

Seth didn't have the authority to commit his paper to any vast expenditure. He told Mrs Oglethorpe that she had been right to come to him first before getting involved with the lower end of the Sunday papers. 'They could well take you for a ride,' he cautioned her. 'Let me see what it is you've got and I'll take it to my Editor so we can see how much your story is worth.'

Whilst Mrs Oglethorpe was something of an innocent abroad on the course she had set herself, she had not come down in the last shower of rain. She knew that if she just handed everything over to Seth Womersely then her negotiating power had gone.

'I'll tell you what I'll do,' she said to Seth. 'You go back to your Editor and tell him I've got all of Old Tom Bones' diaries and that I'll share them with you if the price is right.' She went to her desk and opened a drawer. Seth looked amazed. Before him lay at least twenty volumes of *The Life and Times of Old Tom Bones*.

'Can I take one with me just to prove to the Editor that I've got the genuine article?' Seth asked.

Alice Oglethorpe would have none of it.

It was going to be useless his arguing with Mrs Oglethorpe – he would have to hope that the Editor would trust his judgement. In any event, before any price was agreed they would have to see exactly what it was they were buying. It was with some confidence that he assured Mrs Oglethorpe they could be in business.

As Seth Womersley left – and almost as an aside – he asked Mrs

Oglethorpe how she had come by the diaries.

'That's for me to know and for you not to know,' she replied.

Chapter 11

Arkwright Returns

It had been an anxious time for Doris waiting, as she was, for a phone call from Arkwright. When she had not heard from him by early evening she had become worried that he'd not arrived safely back in the village.

Arkwright had left Chiswick for Kings Cross Station at about half-past nine. They had both checked the times of the trains back north and had calculated that Arkwright would be home by two o'clock, thus giving him ample time to call in to see Mr Grimsdyke at the bank before it closed for the day.

The train had arrived on time and Arkwright's meeting with the bank manager had taken place. But the outcome of that meeting had given Arkwright the mother and father of all headaches. The birth certificate with which he was confronted had certainly not been what he had been expecting.

Arkwright was certainly not going to relate that piece of evidence to Doris when they both knew it to be totally false. In the end he decided to tell Doris on the phone late that evening that nothing so far had been uncovered from the boxes of papers left behind by Old Tom, but that a number of cases had yet to be examined. News should be at hand, he had informed Doris, in a matter of days. Arkwright must have sounded convincing because Doris appeared to accept his story quite happily.

It was with some confidence that Arkwright visited the bank two days later. He was sure that, by now, Mr Grimsdyke would have met up with Old Tom Bones' solicitor and unearthed the information which would shed much needed light on this whole sordid affair. However, movement on that front seemed to have been exceedingly slow due to the fact that Old Tom had not been very methodical in the storing of his papers. When Old Tom's house had been cleared prior to its sale, Mr Grimsdyke had sent the furniture and carpets to the salerooms. All of Old Tom's papers and bric-a-brac had been placed in over fifteen large boxes and these had been sent to Mr Driglington – Old Tom's solicitor – for safekeeping.

Unusually for a solicitor, Mr Driglington had been somewhat tardy in the matter of having the personal papers and effects of Old Tom sorted. A start had been made and the birth certificate found. Thereafter, Mr Driglington had decided to rest on his laurels. After Mr Grimsdyke had related to him his conversation with Arkwright on his return from London, and asked that a further search of the papers to be conducted relating to the birth of Old Tom's child, Ben Driglington had promised to attend to the matter.

But not having heard a word from Ben Driglington, Mr Grimsdyke took it upon himself to enquire directly with him as to the progress being made. It was only after this chase-up call that Mr Driglington bestirred himself – or more accurately, got his managing clerk to rummage through the boxes to see what else they might reveal.

Because professionals tend to cover up for each other, Mr Grimsdyke gave no hint of the incompetence over at the offices of Driglington and Co and merely told Arkwright that nothing useful – so far – had come to light. However, he assured Arkwright that Mr Driglington was 'on the case'. It was against this background that Mr Grimsdyke counselled Arkwright yet again not to disclose to Doris that a second Arkwright was walking on the face of the earth but, rather, just to keep telling her that details were still being awaited from Old Tom Bones' solicitor.

Arkwright was not impressed – nor was he fooled by the line being shot to him by Mr Grimsdyke. 'Old Tom Bones been dead for months now,' Arkwright reminded Mr Grimsdyke. 'How long exactly does it take to look through a few boxes. I've seen people savaged by a dead sheep what are more active than that Ben Driglington. Any solicitor who calls his daughter Sue isn't quite right in the head and I've often had cause to wonder whether the lights are on when you talk to him.'

Mr Driglington had been Arkwright's father's solicitor and he'd had dealings with him when Arkwright Senior had crossed the River Jordan. After being acquainted with the circumstances of the death by the police, Mr Driglington had informed Arkwright that he, too, would like to die peacefully in his sleep as his father had done – rather than screaming and being terrified as were the passengers in his father's car at the time of his death. Arkwright had also been singularly unimpressed at the length of time it had taken Mr Driglington to wind up his father's estate – but then Arkwright had always held most professionals in some contempt since it had dawned on him that the *Titanic* was built by professionals whilst the Ark had been built by amateurs.

Arkwright told Mr Grimsdyke that although he (Arkwright) might not possess any academic qualifications, he'd got more gumption in his little toe than that Bachelor of Laws and Master of Incompetence who was masquerading as a solicitor. 'Doris can't be the mother of Old Tom Bones' child,' he told Mr Grimsdyke, 'because she's been barren since the day she was born. Tell that to Ben Driglington and tell him to start looking for Old Tom Bones' diaries where he wrote down everything.'

Mr Grimsdyke recalled that Doris had told him that it just couldn't be that she was the mother of Old Tom Bones' son but she hadn't presented that particular fact – or any other information – to support her statement. Neither had Arkwright revealed this piece of information when he had been so adamant that the birth certificate just wasn't true. If what Arkwright was now telling him were to be the truth then there was something more to the matter than he had previously supposed.

'Can you substantiate that as a fact?' Mr Grimsdyke asked Arkwright.

'Can I do what?' asked Arkwright who wasn't too strong on long words and who had never caused any man to reach for a dictionary.

Mr Grimsdyke rephrased his question. 'Can it be proved that Doris could never have children.'

'Well, I suppose you'll have to get Doris' permission to speak to her doctor,' Arkwright replied, 'but I think you'll find he'll say that what I'm telling you is right.'

'This certainly puts a different complexion on matters,' Mr Grimsdyke announced. 'Can you get Doris to give me permission to write to her doctor? If it happens that she's not the mother of the child but Old Tom Bones says she was, then the real mother might have an absolute claim on the whole estate.'

Arkwright indicated that he didn't think he would have any problem in getting Doris to agree that her doctor should be contacted – provided it was kept confidential and didn't get put in the papers. 'I don't think Doris would want everybody to know her oven wasn't in full working order, and I don't want that either. I know people talk about us not having any children of our own, and they think it's down to me having no lead in my pencil, but I've been happy to put up with that to save Doris. It's a terrible thing for a woman not to be able to have a baby – it's like going bald. It's all right for a man, but somehow it's not for a woman.'

Mr Grimsdyke began to see Arkwright in a new light after that statement from him. Previously he'd always assumed Arkwright was a gruff, bluff, insensitive Yorkshireman with something of a chauvinistic attitude towards women which suggested he thought than women inferior to men. But here was Arkwright readily accepting having people talk behind his back about his lack of manliness in order to protect his wife. That, thought Mr Grimsdyke, was courage of a rare and high order.

'If Doris wasn't the mother of Old Tom Bones' child, then who was?' Mr Grimsdyke asked.

To that, Arkwright had no answer. 'Perhaps if we read Old Tom Bones' diaries we might find out,' was all Arkwright could suggest.

A phone call was made to the offices of Driglington & Co. When Mr Grimsdyke asked to speak to Ben Driglington he was put through to his secretary, Bella Golightly. 'I'm afraid Mr Driglington is in court all morning,' she informed Mr Grimsdyke, 'and after that he's got a luncheon engagement at the Golf Club.'

'What time do you expect him back from his lunch?' Mr Grimsdyke asked Ms Golightly.

It appeared that lunches at the Golf Club were usually long affairs and, whilst Ms Golightly didn't say so in as many words, the inference was that Mr Driglington's return to the office after such events was not usually marked by a flurry of activity on his part.

'Well,' said Mr Grimsdyke, 'I don't imagine that we should expect any miracles from him this afternoon then. But when he's back in touch with reality can you ask him to look again in the boxes he's holding of Old Tom Bones' papers and see if he can put his hands on Old Tom's diaries. Tell him that I need them very urgently and that I'd be obliged if he would ring me as soon as he's located them.' Ms Golightly assured Mr Grimsdyke that his message would be passed on to her employer.

Chapter 12

Driglington & Co

Ben Driglington was not a recently qualified solicitor. It had been thought that he would retire when his daughter, Sue, had finished her legal education and that he would then leave her to run the firm. But Ben Driglington had hung on in there, much to Sue's considerable dismay.

Whilst Ben was a store of knowledge about the affairs of the people in the upper part of the Widdledale, he was not always quite up-to-date on all aspects of the law. Moreover, the offices of the firm were antiquated. Ben Driglington would have nothing to do with computers, and he rather liked having retained the coal fires in his offices. 'They give the place a friendly feeling,' he'd told Fred Dobbs – his clerk – when he'd complained about the mess they created which it always seemed to be his turn to clear up. Fred had also explained to Mr Driglington on many occasions that he was not too chuffed at having to get the coal in from the yard twice a day. That he also had, daily, to carry the two buckets up to his employer's office situated on the second floor of the premises only added to his sense of grievance.

Papers tied up with red tape littered every office floor, shelf and cupboard. When Mr Grimsdyke had originally phoned Ben Driglington about the contents of Old Tom Bones' boxes and a search had brought forth the birth certificate, it had taken Ben a couple of hours to find them – or, more accurately, for his clerk to find them. Eventually, they were located in the broom cupboard under the stairs. Quite why they had been put there nobody could remember.

49

Fred Dobbs didn't particularly like his employer. But opportunities to work in the law were limited for those who lived in the Dale – unless one was prepared either to move into the town with all of its dirt and petrol fumes, or to travel the thirty miles there daily and thus contribute to the pollution. Fred was too much of a country lover to accept either of the alternatives available to him, and so he had to put up with working for Driglington & Co.

According to Fred, Mr Driglington was so precious that he had often conjectured as to whether Mr Driglington had actually been born or whether he had been knitted by his mother. On a particularly bad day when Mr Driglington had been especially aloof, Fred had commented to one of the secretaries that the boss of the establishment walked as though he had just fouled his pants and looked as though he had just smelt it.

Now Fred had taken something of a shine to Sue, and she found him to be attractive. He wasn't the brightest of articled clerks, having failed his Solicitors' final examinations three times, but he had a ready wit and was courteous in his attention of her. The budding relationship had not escaped Mr Driglington's eyes. On one occasion Fred had been outside Mr Driglington's office when he'd overheard him talking to Sue. 'You invite people like Fred to tea,' he was telling his daughter, 'you don't marry them.' Sue protested that her father was being too harsh on Fred but, after that day, any notion of a continuing romantic attachment between the two of them was consigned to the dustbin.

Not that Mr Driglington couldn't find anything good to say about Fred. He considered Fred to be totally unspoilt by failure and one who could make a good cup of tea – and, no less importantly, get a coal fire started on a cold frosty morning faster than Baden Powell could have done whenever he'd had got two boy scouts to rub together.

The very thought of having to search again through Old Tom Bones' papers and memorabilia didn't exactly appeal to Fred. Old Tom's armpits and feet had been legend throughout the Dale and Fred couldn't contain a slight shiver going down his spine as he contemplated having to put his hands in the boxes. Nevertheless, the job had to be done and, at least, he knew that he was principally searching for Old Tom's diaries. If these could be located speedily then it might not be necessary for him to put his hands on the microbe infested mass of papers now being committed to him for close scrutiny.

As he approached the first box, Fred thought he was on a mission like opening Joanna Southcott's chest of eternal truth. The first box, when opened, wasn't accompanied (as he had feared) by the release of a swarm of trapped flies which had incubated whilst being stored in the warm offices of Driglington & Co. Indeed, the box – whilst containing a muddle of papers – was almost clean. But of the diaries, there was no sight. A search of all the other boxes failed to produce a single diary.

To sort out the masses of papers was clearly going to take a considerable time. Some – such as old bills all dutifully marked 'paid' and dated together with the cheque number discharging the debt – could be put on one side for immediate incineration. However, it would be necessary to read each of the letters and other documents to see if they merited retention.

But before starting on that Herculean task, Fred thought he had best appraise Mr Driglington of the fact that no diaries could be found. Being 'cup of tea' time, Fred acquainted his employer of his discoveries – or lack of discovery – as he delivered Mr Driglington his mid-morning beverage.

With much tut tutting Mr Driglington told Fred he would contact Mr Grimsdyke at the bank to see if he could remember having seen the diaries when he'd cleared Old Tom Bones' house. In the meantime, he told Fred that he should return to the boxes and begin to put the papers into appropriate piles – and to keep a weather look out for anything which might shed any light on the son Old Tom Bones said that he had fathered.

When the point was directly addressed to him, Mr Grimsdyke had to own up to not remembering whether or not he had actually seen Old Tom Bones' diaries when he had cleared his house. According to Arkwright, if Old Tom Bones had meticulously recorded all the events of his life – or even those of the last twenty years – then there would have been a tidy stack of books to have been collected together. Surely, Mr Grimsdyke reasoned with himself, he could not have helped but notice them. Indeed, had they been there he would probably have looked at some of them whilst the removal men had gone about their business. It was with some – if not absolute – certainty that Mr Grimsdyke reported to Mr Driglington that none of the diaries was in the house when it was cleared of its contents. The only question to be asked now was, *where had they gone?*

Clearly, there had been no burglary at Old Tom's house because no items of value had been stolen. Moreover, Old Tom Bones' house was in the middle of the village and anybody entering it would have been observed by Mrs Troughton who lived next door, and whose face was almost as much a fixture to her windows as were her perpetually undrawn curtains. Whilst we, dear readers, know who it was who had taken the diaries, it was not a piece of intelligence known at that time by either Mr Grimsdyke or Mr Driglington. The matter was of some concern to them – and it was a matter of even greater concern when they knew what had actually happened to them.

It was about mid-afternoon that Fred Dobbs presented himself again in the office of Mr Driglington. Fred was waving a piece of paper in his hand. 'I think this might be what we are looking for,' he announced.

Mr Driglington and Fred Dobbs

52

Chapter 13

The Editor's Desk

Seth Womersley had spoken to his Editor about Alice Oglethorpe. She was not a woman to whom he had warmed, but she had a story. And to a reporter, it's the story that counts – especially when it's dynamite.

It has to be said that Alice Oglethorpe was not a popular figure in the village. Possessed of a bungalow mind, she had the facial features of one which looked as though it would eat its young. But her audience in the village was increasing as she began to reveal, little bit by little bit, what she had read in Old Tom Bones' diaries. Not that Mrs Oglethorpe ever revealed the source of her information.

It had been arranged that Seth would collect Mrs Oglethorpe from her home so that she could take to the Editor of the *Widdledale Gazette* the diaries now in her possession. He would then judge their worth and make an offer of funds to her for their immediate possession.

Mrs Oglethorpe didn't have much idea as to the amount she should hold out for, but she did know that the figure should have four noughts on the end. The negotiable part was the first digit of the sum.

She didn't want to appear greedy. After all, she did have some principles – but, on the other hand, she thought that when the whole story came out in the wash she might have to leave the village and she would need a comfortable resettlement allowance. For no particular reason, she decided to hang her hat on five thousand pounds.

Over at the *Gazette*, Seth and his Editor were also contemplating figures. 'The story's worth a fortune for us if we can get a lead into the Sunday papers,' Seth said. 'What we need to do is see the diaries, investigate them and then syndicate the story.'

The Editor thought for a moment. 'Let's see if we can get her to suggest a figure, then we'll knock her down a bit,' he said to Seth. With the game plan made, Seth set out to collect the Werewolf of Widdledale.

Only Mrs Troughton observed Alice Oglethorpe, weighed down by a suitcase, as she got into Seth's car. It struck Mrs Troughton as odd that Mrs Oglethorpe should be dressed up and packed up as if she were going on holiday without having told anybody in the village that she was going away. It seemed even stranger that Seth Womersley was being used to ferry her to the railway station when everybody in the village always used Harry Robertshaw's taxi service. 'No matter,' Mrs Troughton told her cat, Lucifer, 'the way that woman's been behaving lately it's best she's gone away.'

With the formalities of shaking of hands concluded at the offices of the *Gazette*, the Editor asked Alice Oglethorpe to show him some of the diaries. 'I can't tell you whether they're worth anything until I've had a good look at them,' he told Mrs Oglethorpe.

'But if I show you them and you say they aren't worth anything there's nothing to stop you publishing later what you've seen without having given me a penny,' Mrs Oglethorpe replied.

'Now, Mrs Oglethorpe,' the Editor responded. 'We don't do business like that at the *Gazette*. You can trust us. I promise that if we tell you that the diaries are of no use to us then we won't print anything you've shown us unless the information comes to us from a different source.'

Mrs Oglethorpe hesitated for a moment and then pulled out a diary from her case. 'I think this might convince you,' she said to the Editor. 'Look at the entries here.'

Alice Oglethorpe opened the diary for the Editor and Seth to read. What they saw took them by surprise. Certainly, neither of them had previously even imagined what was being revealed to them.

'Well, Mrs Oglethorpe,' the Editor said, 'I think you may have something here with might be of interest to us. The paper will have to consult its solicitor before it can publish this information, but I think we could have a deal if we can agree on a price. Have you a figure in mind?'

What the Editor did not tell Mrs Oglethorpe was that she could well find herself in a sticky legal position if it were ever discovered that she didn't have legal ownership of the diaries. And if, in that connection, the *Gazette* were obliged to disclose who was the provider of the information it had published, then it would have to do so.

Mrs Oglethorpe could see from the reaction on the faces of Seth Womersley and the Editor that they liked what they had seen and were probably very keen to get hold of all the diaries. Her original idea of five thousand pounds might, she now thought, be somewhat on the low side. Whether she was thought greedy or not did worry her now. 'Ten thousand pounds is the price,' she announced firmly.

Seth and the Editor were somewhat taken aback. Whilst they knew that the story the diaries revealed would nett them a considerable sum, ten thousand pounds was a far higher price than they had considered they would have to pay. They had to admire Mrs Oglethorpe's entrepreneurial spirit and imagination.

'That's very considerably in excess of what we had in mind,' the Editor told Mrs Oglethorpe. 'We had a figure of just a few hundred pounds marked down for the diaries. However, now that we've seen what's actually on offer, I think we could go up to four hundred pounds – but even then, that's a lot for what you have to offer.'

'Perhaps I should see what the *News of the World* might offer?' Mrs Oglethorpe replied.

'Well, that's entirely up to you,' said the Editor. 'But once you get those boys into the action they'll start muckraking around everywhere – including digging up information about you. You wouldn't want that, would you?'

'I've nothing to hide,' Mrs Oglethorpe said briskly, 'but those press people do sometimes twist things round, which you've said, and I don't want my face being published the length and breadth of the country.'

'Quite so,' said the Editor. 'How about I go up to four hundred and fifty pounds – in cash or a cheque, here and now.'

The sum was well below what Alice Oglethorpe had hoped for and it didn't look as though her original ball park figure was going to be reached. 'Make it six hundred pounds and you've got a deal – and if it's cash you're offering I'll leave the diaries with you now.'

The Editor and Seth went into a huddle and pretended to be arguing about the sum. Finally the Editor said, 'You've got a deal if you'll settle at five hundred pounds.' The deal was struck as he stood up and shook hands with Mrs Oglethorpe. With his other hand, he deftly lifted up the suitcase and handed it to Seth.

Diaries and cash exchanged hands. The suitcase might now have been pounds lighter in weight but it was pounds heavier in notes of the realm – even if significantly fewer than Alice Oglethorpe had hoped for when she had set off for her meeting at the *Gazette.*

Seth escorted Mrs Oglethorpe to his car and returned her home. Only Mrs Troughton seated by the window saw Mrs Oglethorpe return. 'That was a short holiday,' she confided in Lucifer.

Once inside her house, Mrs Oglethorpe began the task of hiding the money in secret places around the house. 'You can't trust nobody these days not to steal from you,' she said to herself.

Back at the *Gazette*, the Editor and Seth discussed their deal.

'Do you think you should have warned Mrs Oglethorpe that the nationals will get hold of this story and that when they do, they'll be all over her?' Seth asked.

'I don't think so,' the Editor replied. 'It'll teach her that when she sups with the devil she needs a very long spoon. If the press crucify her, then she's only going to get what she deserves. As far as Old Tom Bones and his relationship with Mrs Oglethorpe is concerned, she's displayed all the characteristics of his foul smelling dog except loyalty. Anyway, we've got work to do. To start with we need a legal opinion as to what we can publish without getting into trouble.

'Get the diaries down to Tom Driglington and see what he's got to say about them.'

Chapter 14

Investigative Journalism

Before Seth Womersley took the diaries to Ben Driglington he thought he should skim through the pages relating to the time Old Tom Bones had said Doris Broughton had born him a son.

The entries in the diary revealed quite clearly that Old Tom knew that Doris wasn't the mother of the child in question and that, of this son, Little Bessie Sidebottom was really the mother. But the diaries also revealed that Old Tom wasn't actually the father. Who the real father would have become apparent to Seth if he had only read on. But the parts he had read caused his eyes to open wide. He was acutely aware that if he revealed what he now knew, then good and honest Dalesfolk might well suffer both embarrassment and great personal hurt. But for Seth, truth mattered and a story was a story that had to be told – especially if it were one which would advance his career in journalism. He convinced himself – quite easily as it happened – that, no matter what the temporary difficulties certain people in the village and in Wellerby might face, the greater would be the good for all concerned if the truth be told – provided it were told with compassion.

As Seth read the diaries he came across the name of Betty Entwistle to whom glowing tributes were paid for her steadfast friendship towards Doris. The address book section of the diary revealed her address in Chiswick.

Seth knew that Doris had disappeared without trace. None of his informants had heard sound of her anywhere in the Dale and he knew of Doris' aversion of ever leaving the place of her birth. Seth may have only possessed a worthless GNVQ, but he was willing to bet his next pay cheque (not that it amounted to much) that Doris was now in London. And that idea fitted in nicely as an explanation for Arkwright's recent one night of absence from the village.

Seth did consider seeking out Arkwright and confronting him directly with his theory that he'd been to the nation's capital city but he decided the greater drama would be in first confronting Doris in London with the story he was about to unfold in the *Gazette*.

By now the paper had purchased a new camera. Seth didn't want to take the *Gazette*'s photographer with him to London, and he wanted to see Doris before he saw Mr Driglington. It was also important to Seth that his Editor didn't know what he was up to. This was going to be Seth's big story and he wanted the full credit and glory of it all for himself.

It took some courage on his part to lie to his Editor when he had told him that Ben Driglington was out of the office for a few days but an appointment had been made for them to meet the following week. Seth had just to hope that his Editor and Mr Driglington wouldn't have a chance encounter before he got back from London.

Seth told his Editor that he needed a couple of days off to go to London on some personal business, but that he would use the occasion to the benefit of the *Gazette* by writing a story about his trip. Seth said he believed the story would be all the better if he could have some photographs to go with it. With dire warnings of the consequences to his pay packet if the camera were not returned in full working order, the Editor gave his blessing to Seth's outing to London. The experience, he thought, would do the lad good as, heretofore, Seth had never been further afield than Leeds.

The journey to London was uneventful. His heart had skipped a beat when he had seen in the distance the ground where Arsenal played. Leeds United, Seth thought, were a group of whingers who were frequently outclassed by the superior skills of Arsenal. Not that he'd ever dared venture that opinion in the Cat and Fiddle on a Saturday night.

Although Seth had never been to London before, he was better acquainted with what to expect than had been Arkwright. Whilst there, indeed, were massage parlours in Leeds, Seth had formed the

58

opinion that the masseuses there would be innocents abroad when compared with what would be on offer London. In this respect he was to be disappointed. A 'full body massage' was no different from those he'd experienced up north – except for the price. The biggest relief he experienced from his massage was mainly the extra twenty pounds it cost for what was on offer in Leeds City Square.

Whilst it is true that the built up frustrations from his train journey to London had been ameliorated, Seth did not believe the expenditure had been justified. There would be no pics in his story for the *Gazette* of Madam Fifi at La Maison de la Coeur. A somewhat wiser and less rich man, he boarded the tube to Chiswick.

Seth saw the flat in nearby Brentford where Mandy Rice Davis had once lived, and he also took a picture of the garage in Chiswick High Road where the Great Train Robbers had bought a car. The Gunnersbury Flyover also merited a picture, as did the Express where he had a bar lunch prior to taking a leisurely stroll on the bridge across the Thames as he ambled amiably towards Kew Gardens. Not that Seth knew anything about gardening – but the pictures would look good in the *Gazette* for its readers in the Dale for whom the growing of daffodils and tulips was a horticultural orgasm.

And then Seth went about his job of facing up to Doris. He wondered if she really knew the truth of the matter and, if not, how she would react to the story he was about to reveal to her.

Did she know – or had she already guessed? – that Arkwright was the real father of the child that had dropped from the loins of Little Bessie Sidebottom. Or were the revelations in Old Toms' diaries a mischief on his part to get even with Doris for her having spurned his love for her? He was about to find out.

Seth rang the doorbell of 103 Chiswick High Road, a large Victorian house now divided into four flats. There was no reply. He would have to try again later. In the meantime he needed to find some lodgings for the night. He saw a McDonald's on a street corner where he ordered fillet o' fish. He asked for it to be served without the tartar sauce for which he substituted tomato sauce.

He enquired of a passing waitress if she knew of a place where he could rest his head for the night. When she realised he wasn't being forward she gave him directions.

Half an hour later he pressed a doorbell. A lady called Maggie opened the door.

Chapter 15

Maggie, as recommended by McDonald's

As Seth completed the booking-in procedures at Maggie's place, Maggie remarked to him that she'd had a lodger about a week ago who spoke just like him. With those words, Seth believed he'd struck gold.

'Where was he from?' Seth asked.

'Oh, some place called Widdledale. I'd never heard of it but he told me it was somewhere in Yorkshire.'

Seth admitted that he was also from the Dale, and it didn't take long after that for the ace investigative journalist to confirm that it was, indeed, Arkwright who'd been a resident at the Dunham Massey Guest House but a few days ago.

'Arkwright and me,' Seth said, 'know each other well. I think he was down here to see his wife, wasn't he?'

'That's right,' said Maggie, 'but I didn't think anybody up there in Yorkshire knew that he'd come down here to find her.'

'Well, me and Arkwright go back a long way,' Seth lied. 'He didn't want people to know where Doris was because there's been a lot of nasty chattering going on about her in the Dale since she's been left a lot of money in a Will. But he'd confided in me and said he was coming down to Chiswick to get matters put right so she could come back home. Have you heard from him since he went back, because I seem to remember him saying to me that he was coming to see Doris again?'

Seth's nose was beginning to grow an inch longer with each statement he made.

'No, he's not been in contact with me since he went back up north,' Maggie said. 'Perhaps next time he's down here he'll be staying with Doris at her friend's house. It's all such a sad affair – Arkwright seemed such a nice chap and from what he told me about Doris she sounds like a woman in a million.'

'A woman in three million,' Seth said, trying to appear witty and funny; but Maggie didn't laugh.

'Yes,' said Seth, 'Doris is a very special person.'

Whilst Seth knew of Doris, his actual knowledge of her was no more than that which any gash reporter would have had who was only aware of the names of the central characters in the several villages in the Dale. Seth couldn't recall having ever spoken to Doris. Indeed, had it not been for the fact that he'd seen a photograph of Doris on the sideboard when he'd called on Arkwright shortly after the terms of the Will had been published in the *Gazette*, he doubted if he'd have been able to recognise Doris in the flesh when he'd called to see her at Betty Entwistle's house.

'Yes,' Seth continued, 'she's a grand woman and we're all missing her very much. I often called in on her when I was in the village and, as often as not, I'd be prevailed upon to stay for tea.'

Seth rubbed his nose – just in case.

'What do you do in the Dale?' Maggie asked. Seth couldn't tell her that he was an ace investigative reporter, otherwise it would be odds-on that Maggie would clam up on him. Moreover, he didn't think she'd take too kindly to having been duped into talking to him about Arkwright.

'I'm a chartered accountant,' he told Maggie. He hadn't wanted to appear too grand in his invention and it had been a toss up between telling her he was an accountant or an estate agent.

Not that Seth ever had any head for figures. In maths classes at Junior school he'd always had trouble with mensuration and, when he'd told his mother, she told him not to talk mucky.

Maggie, though, was impressed. 'Perhaps you can help me with my tax return?' she asked.

Seth laughed. 'I'm a bit out of date on taxation,' he said, 'I tend to specialise in corporate acquisitions and merges these days.' Seth didn't have a clue what he was talking about and he was reasonably confident that neither would Maggie – but she did look impressed.

'Ah well,' said Maggie, 'I'll have to struggle with it on my own like I've always done.'

'I haven't seen Arkwright since he got back to the Dale,' Seth said. 'Did he seem in good spirits after he'd seen Doris?'

Maggie wasn't able to say and she explained to Seth that Arkwright had only stayed the night, and that in the morning when he left to see Doris he'd taken his case with him so he'd be able to go straight back north after seeing her. 'I don't know what happened when he saw his beloved Doris, but he was very apprehensive about the meeting. He told me quite a lot when we had dinner together, but I don't think he thought he was talking to me in confidence. And that didn't matter to him because he never expected to come across me again.'

There was a lull in the conversation. Seth started the chatter again desperately trying to get Maggie to talk to him about Arkwright. But she would have none of it. Perhaps, Seth thought, she's had a woman's intuition that he wasn't quite the person he was representing himself to be. The ace investigative journalist had come to a full stop.

'What are you going to do tomorrow?' Maggie asked Seth.

'Oh, nothing in particular,' Seth replied. 'I think I'll see some of the sights of London before I go back home.'

'What made you come to Chiswick in the first place?' Maggie asked.

Seth was beginning to feel that he was not on very safe ground. He had to think fast.

'Well,' he responded, 'it's really quite by chance that I ended up here rather than actually in London. On the train down I read an article about Chiswick House and I thought that I'd rather like to see it – not that I know anything about architecture or pictures, but it'll do me good to have a bit of culture and it'll make a change from corporate acquisitions and mergers. Who knows, perhaps one of my clients might like to acquire the property.'

'I don't think you'll find its for sale,' Maggie replied.

Seth began to get quite keen to get away from Maggie now that her questions were beginning to flow quick and fast. She was becoming too much like an investigative journalist. So he stretched his legs and suggested that he take himself out of his chair and go for a short walk, to look around the place, before turning in for the night.

'It's a nice walk down by Strand on the Green and you'll see the Thames,' Maggie suggested. 'And there are a couple of nice pubs there if you feel like a drink.'

Immediately Seth was out of the house, Maggie went to her Visitors' Register and turned the pages backwards. There she found Arkwright's number. Seconds later Arkwright was answering his phone.

'It's Maggie here,' she said. 'Do you remember that you stayed at my guest house in Chiswick a few days ago?'

Arkwright did indeed remember. They exchanged a few pleasantries and then Maggie told him that his friend Seth Womersley was staying with her for the night. A long silence followed.

'Are you still there?' Maggie asked.

Arkwright was stunned. 'What's that waste of skin up to?' he asked Maggie.

Maggie said that Seth had told her that he was a chartered accountant and that he was a big friend of his but that she'd got a bit suspicious when he kept pumping her for information about him and his meeting with Doris.

'I didn't tell him anything,' Maggie assured Arkwright, 'but I think he'll be making a call on Doris tomorrow morning.'

Arkwright agreed with Maggie that would probably be the sole purpose of his visit to London. 'I'll get on to Doris straight away,' he told Maggie, and he thanked her for tipping him off. 'Don't let him know that you've spoken to me,' he added as an afterthought.

Maggie asked if he was planning to come to London again and Arkwright told her that he would be – but it wouldn't be for a few days as certain matters were still outstanding. 'When they're cleared up I'll be down to collect Doris to bring her back home.' Arkwright promised that if the opportunity arose he would call in to see her.

Arkwright was anxious to speak to Doris as quickly as possible. His conversation with Maggie had therefore to be cut short. Mutual 'bye-byes' were expressed and within seconds Arkwright was speaking with Doris.

Doris was dismayed at what Arkwright was telling her but she assured him that she would never speak to Seth. After he had rung off, Doris told her friend Betty what had happened. 'We can sort that out quite easily,' Betty told Doris.

The following morning, as surely as night follows day, Seth Womersley was once again ringing the doorbell of 103 Chiswick High Road. And for the second time there was no answer. Drastic action was needed. Seth pressed the doorbell again and kept his finger on the little white button. A figure appeared at the door whom Seth assumed would be Betty Entwistle.

'Hello, Betty,' Seth said presumptuously. 'Is Doris in?'

'I'm not Betty,' the lady announced fiercely, 'she lives in the next flat to me and I'll ask you kindly never to ring her doorbell in that manner again. Anyway, you can't see either of them because they've gone away for a few days.'

Seth apologised for the inconvenience he'd caused and walked away.

As he turned and looked backwards at the house he was certain he saw the curtains twitch. Now he knew Maggie had rumbled him and he was not looking forward to collecting his belongings from the Dunham Massey Guest House. And he was most certainly not looking forward to his next meeting with Arkwright Broughton.

Chapter 16

An Opinion is Needed

It was with some trepidation that Seth Womersley returned to his desk after his trip to London. He was aware that he would be for the high jump if the Editor had chanced to meet up with Ben Driglington during his absence. Explanations would have been demanded as to why he hadn't, as clearly instructed, seen the solicitor immediately about his legal opinion of the diaries. And there was the added complication that Seth hadn't bothered to mention to the Editor that he was going to try and find Doris whilst he was in London.

The gods had smiled on Seth. There was no note awaiting him on his desk summoning him to appear before the editorial chair.

It was the following morning that Seth kept his appointment with Mr Driglington. The *Gazette* paid Driglington & Co a monthly retainer fee. Thus far in that relationship the paper had only once had to use the firm in a legal matter – and that on the relatively trivial issue of chasing up an advertiser who was showing a determined reluctance not to pay a long outstanding bill. The Editor, therefore, thought his legal eagles were quids in on the deal which had been struck between them. Whenever Ben Driglington took a holiday in the winter to warmer climes, the Editor was known to observe that it was his paper which was funding the vacation in the sun. However, now was the time that the paper was going to get its money's worth from Ben Driglington.

For Seth Womersley, a trip to the offices of Driglington & Co was like stepping back in time. It wasn't just the old coal fires in the offices but, rather, the gas mantles used to illuminate the rooms.

Ben Driglington did once consider converting his lighting system to electricity but had decided it would have been an unnecessary extravagance to do so. Seth vowed that, one day, he would write an article for the *Gazette* on the museum piece of an office which quite fascinated him. But he was not visiting the solicitor today for a conducted tour down memory lane.

Fred Dobbs ushered Seth into Mr Driglington's office. Seth carefully placed the diaries on the expansive desk of the solicitor and announced that they were the diaries of the late Old Tom Bones which, subject to his legal opinion, the *Gazette* was going to publish over a number of weeks.

An enormous frown covered Ben Driglington's face as he picked up one of the diaries and peered inside it through the half-moon, gold-rimmed spectacles perched on the end of his nose. They were certainly written in Old Tom Bones' hand and, *prima facie*, it would appeared that they were indeed his missing diaries.

'The presence of these diaries,' said Mr Driglington as he rose from his chair and walked to stand with his back to the open fire in his office, 'presents me with a problem. I, and my father before me, have been the solicitors for the late Mr Bones for the past forty years and I am involved with Mr Grimsdyke in winding up the affairs and the estate of Mr Thomas Bones.

'These diaries which you have placed before me, and what had happened to them, has been a matter which has exercised the minds of both Mr Grimsdyke and myself for the past few weeks. There is no record that the late Mr Bones ever gave the diaries away and a situation arises which suggests that they must have been stolen. I could ask you how they have come to be in the possession of the *Gazette* but if I were to do so, I would have to advise you, as your paper's solicitor, not to answer that question. However, I should appraise you of the very distinct possibility that, at some time in the very near future, the police might be involved to ascertain your legal title to these pieces of property. *Nemo dat quod non habet* are words which spring to my mind.'

'We talk of little else at the *Gazette*,' said Seth trying to make light of his lack of knowledge of Latin.

Mr Driglington returned slowly to his desk and leant back in his large green leather swivel chair. He looked to the ceiling and became much involved in his own thoughts. Such was his stillness and for so long that Seth began to wonder whether Mr Driglington was still of this world. But Mr Driglington was still in this world, if not quite of it. He was pondering the dilemma which faced him.

For the first part, he was paid a retainer fee by the *Gazette* and he was thus obliged to offer advice to the paper under the terms of the contract which existed between them – which terms would certainly include a matter of this nature. For the second part, he was being retained by the Bank to deal with the legal work involved in winding up Old Tom Bones' estate. Here was a conflict of interest, the like of which he had never come across before in his entire legal career.

In the fullness of time Mr Driglington returned to Mother Earth and turned his gaze on Seth who, by now, was somewhat at a loss to comprehend what was happening.

'I think,' Mr Driglington continued in his very formal mode of speech, 'that issues unbeknownst to the *Gazette* require that I speak urgently and directly to your Editor, for I am not certain that I am in a position to act for your paper in this matter. Indeed, before I proceed further I, too, may need to take some legal advice. All that I can say now is that you must take these diaries away and put them in a safe place and I counsel you to do nothing further with them for the time being.'

Seth looked puzzled. He saw no problems. The paper had bought the diaries and, whilst it might be questionable as to how fairly they had dealt with Mrs Oglethorpe, the transaction was no different from those made by other newspapers everywhere, every day. As far as Seth was concerned the diaries were not stolen property. But Seth was not learned in the law and he felt himself in no position to debate the matter with Mr Driglington. Accordingly, he informed the solicitor that he would report back to his Editor and ask that he get in touch with him immediately.

Seth collected up the diaries and made towards the door. 'What was that you said?' Seth asked Mr Driglington, 'never quod the habit?'

Mr Driglington smiled a superior smile. 'You can never give a better title than that which you inherit,' he replied.

Seth was none the wiser but he allowed his facial features to pretend that a great legal truth had dawned upon him.

On his way back to the *Gazette*, Seth saw Mrs Oglethorpe enter Edwin Pickles' Emporium – which was the nearest thing the small Dale's town had to a supermarket. As a piece of architecture the building was a monstrosity and totally out of keeping with the properties which surrounded it. How planning permission had ever been obtained for its erection was a mystery. But there this single storey building was – known irreverently to all and sundry in the Dale as Edwin's Little Erection.

The idea of calling the shop an Emporium had come to Edwin Pickles after he had read *Kipps*. To Edwin, the name Emporium suggested times past when shop assistants knew their place and served their customers with the respect and servile courtesy expected of them. Whereas in the past the small town had separate shops for the butcher, baker, grocer, ironmonger, haberdasher, post office and the sweetie shop selling tobacco and papers, all of these units of retailing were now housed under one roof – Edwin's roof. Those old enough to remember sawdust on the floor of grocer's shops felt comfortable in Edwin's Emporium, whilst the younger generation saw such features in a shop as something of a novelty. All that was missing was a penny's worth of dolly mixtures being served up in paper rolled into a cornet shape by an obliging shop assistant.

Seth followed Mrs Oglethorpe into the Emporium hoping that he could contrive to bump into her by accident. He bought a loaf of bread and went to stand behind Mrs Oglethorpe in the butchery department.

Mrs Oglethorpe turned to speak to him. 'When will you start publishing the diaries?' she asked.

'Well, we've got to read through them all first,' Seth replied, 'but it won't take long now. Do you mind if we give you a bit of praise when we print them and say how indebted we are to you for letting us have them?' As an afterthought Seth added that, of course, the *Gazette* would not mention they had paid her for the diaries.

That was not an outcome Mrs Oglethorpe had ever envisaged when she had sold the diaries to the *Gazette*. But it didn't take her long to come up with a sharp 'No thank you'. She bought a lamb chop and before Seth could engage her further in conversation she bid him a 'Good morning' and was away off out of the Emporium.

When Seth eventually got back to the *Gazette* he told the Editor of the odd meeting he'd had with Mr Driglington – the upshot of which seemed to be that if you didn't have a title to your name then you couldn't have the diaries. The Editor asked Seth to talk more sense but all he could add was that Mr Driglington had asked him to get his boss to give him a bell to make an appointment for them to meet as soon as possible – and that in the meantime they hadn't to publish anything from the diaries.

As an afterthought, Seth told his Editor that Mr Driglington had seemed put out at seeing the diaries and that he appeared to believe they were the stolen property of one of his clients – albeit a deceased one.

The Editor was unimpressed by what his employee was telling him. 'We pay that chap Driglington a retainer every month,' he said, 'so he can't just dump us like that. Anyway, what's all this about the diaries being stolen? Tell me again, precisely what did Mrs Oglethorpe tell you when you asked her how she had come by the diaries?'

'She said, "That's for me to know and for you not to know,"' Seth replied, 'so I didn't press her on the point.' The Editor shook his head in disbelief at his reporter's lack of investigative reporting techniques.

'I think you might have got us into a spot of bother here,' the Editor told Seth. 'I suppose we can always refuse to say how the diaries came into our possession, and I don't imagine that Mrs Oglethorpe is going to shout it from the rooftops that she sold them to us. We'll just have to sit it out and see what develops. For heaven's sake, if anybody asks you anything just say that you have "no comment".'

The phone rang in the Editor's office.

'Arkwright Broughton on the phone to speak to you,' announced the switchboard operator.

'Can you tell him that I'm tied up at the moment but that I'll call him back later today?' The instruction was carried out.

'That was Arkwright Broughton on the phone,' the Editor

informed Seth. 'I wonder what bit of information he's got for us now? I'll ring him back after I've spoken with Ben Driglington.'

Seth guessed he knew full well the purpose of the call. It did occur to him to make a full confession there and then to his Editor but he took that view that he who runs away lives to fight another day. Unlikely though it may be, perhaps Arkwright was phoning about something other than the failed visit of the *Gazette*'s ace investigative reporter to Doris at her temporary abode in Chiswick. It was a desperate hope. But it is in desperate situations that one is sustained by hope. Seth kept quiet and made a hurried excuse to make a hurried departure from the Editor's office.

The Editor phoned Mr Driglington. 'Did you have a nice few days away last week?' began the Editor.

The Editor was taken aback to be told by Mr Driglington that he hadn't been away from his office in ages.

'I think we'd better meet to discuss the situation over the diaries your lad brought round to my office earlier today,' Ben Driglington told the Editor. 'I've got a space in my diary at two this afternoon. Can you call in on me then?'

The Editor consulted his diary. 'That's fine with me,' he said. 'Now, what's all this about these diaries being stolen and your not being able to advise us about publishing them?'

'I think we'd best talk about that this afternoon,' replied Mr Driglington.

Chapter 17

Arkwright gets Annoyed

A week had passed since Arkwright had been in conversation with Mr Grimsdyke. The promise that Mr Driglington was 'on the case' in the matter of searching for Old Tom's diaries amongst the papers deposited at the offices of Driglington & Co didn't seem to have amounted to much in his eyes. Moreover, Arkwright had been more than a little put out when he had discovered that the *Gazette*'s ace investigative reporter had been attempting to harass Doris. Action was needed – and needed fast.

'Things have got to start happening,' Arkwright demanded of Mr Grimsdyke. 'You and Ben Driglington hold the key to this bloody puzzle and I want it sorted.' To emphasise the point, Arkwright thumped the bank manager's desk – which rather startled Mr Grimsdyke. Most visitors to his office were trembling supplicants seeking a compassionate understanding of their worsening overdraft position. Nobody ever before had thumped his desk. And it wasn't just Mr Grimsdyke who had jumped – his cup and saucer had fair rattled at the physical assault on his desk.

In truth, Mr Grimsdyke was disappointed that Ben Driglington had not been in touch with him, and the bank manager felt a slight pang of guilt that he had done so little to chase up the solicitor.

'You have a fair point,' Mr Grimsdyke said to Arkwright as he tried to mollify him. 'This whole matter has dragged on for far too long and I'm sorry that it hasn't been sorted.'

Mr Grimsdyke was mindful of the possible damage being done to the bank's reputation for efficiency. If he were not seen to be doing things right now then, when Doris Broughton actually came into Old Tom Bones' money, she might well seek to find another custodian of the funds. Then, the profits which Mr Grimsdyke had previously anticipated would come his branch's way would go elsewhere, and Head Office would be far from being best pleased with him for losing such an important customer. Reflecting on that situation, it wasn't only Arkwright who was now beginning to feel annoyed.

'I'll get on to Ben Driglington right now,' Mr Grimsdyke said, 'and I'll let you have the extension to my phone so that you can hear what he's got to say for himself.'

Arkwright picked up his handset immediately Mr Grimsdyke was through to the offices of Driglington & Co.

'Now then, Ben,' Mr Grimsdyke began, 'what's the news on these diaries you're supposed to be looking for amongst Old Tom Bones' papers?'

'Well,' replied the solicitor, 'I can tell you that they're not with the papers you sent round to me after we cleared out Old Tom Bones' house.'

Mr Grimsdyke remarked rather tersely that he wished Ben Driglington had told him that as soon as he had known they were not in his possession. 'If they're not with the papers you took away from Old Tom Bones' house, have you any clue as to where they might be now?'

'Now that's a question which occasions me a great difficulty,' Mr Driglington replied in his usual pompous style. He could, of course, have lied and told the bank manager that he had no idea where the diaries were but, sooner or later, they were going to be discovered – at which time enquiries would be made as to how they had got into the hands of the *Gazette* and it would come to light that, at one stage, the diaries had actually reposed on his desk. When that happened, Mr Grimsdyke (for whom he was acting in a legal capacity in the winding up of Old Tom Bones' estate) could put some awkward question to the Law Society demanding to know why he had held back important information from him. The thought of facing a Disciplinary Panel held no appeal to Ben Driglington in the suppertime of his legal career.

'What do you mean, it's a difficult question for you to answer?' Mr Grimsdyke asked. 'Either you've got some idea as to where the diaries might be, or you haven't.'

It was only Mr Grimsdyke's giving of urgent hand signals to Arkwright that kept him from an intemperate outburst. The veins on Arkwright's head stood out like rivers about to burst their banks.

'All I can say at the moment is that I can't say anything at the moment concerning the whereabouts of the diaries,' Ben Driglington replied.

'But that means you know something, doesn't it?' Mr Grimsdyke persisted.

'I cannot say anything more at the moment,' was the firm and unequivocal response from the solicitor.

Mr Grimsdyke scribbled a message on a piece of paper and slid it over his desk to Arkwright. It told him to be absolutely quiet as he questioned Ben Driglington further. Arkwright nodded his head in agreement.

'Look,' said Mr Grimsdyke, 'surely you can tell me something off the record. We're both involved in winding up Mr Bones' estate and I'll treat what you tell me in total confidence. You do know where the diaries are, don't you?'

Ben Driglington was in something of a quandary. He wanted to tell Mr Grimsdyke what he knew about the diaries but to do so would breach his terms of duty towards the *Gazette*. What he had been shown by Seth Womersley was privileged information and could not be disclosed to a third party without the *Gazette*'s permission. But he also had a duty of care both to the late Tom Bones and to the bank – both parties being his clients and both having an interest in the diaries, even if one of them was of a non-corporeal state.

It is not entirely unknown in legal situations that sometimes a confidence could be shared under Chatham House Rules and Ben Driglington had to decide, on the spot, whether this could be one of those times.

'I know what you're saying,' he told Mr Grimsdyke. 'Under different circumstances I might, perhaps, be able to share a confidence with you on this matter but as things currently stand I can say no more than that which I've already told you.'

The veins in Arkwright's neck and on his head looked as though he was going to burst as they pulsated like an African jungle drum – but he was mindful of the undertaking he had given to Mr Grimsdyke and he held his peace.

Mr Grimsdyke made one last attempt to solicit the desired information from Ben Driglington but the message which came back was a resounding, 'No comment.'

'Well, this puts me in a difficult position,' Mr Grimsdyke told Ben Driglington. 'Clearly you do know something which you're not going to tell me. It's certainly not a state of affairs which I'm happy about when we're supposed to be working together. If necessary I'll have to take you to court to get information from you – nothing personal you understand.'

Ben Driglington could only say that what had to be done would have to be done. He did, however, ask the bank manager if he could give him until lunchtime the following day before he took any action. Mr Driglington had in mind that he would be seeing the Editor of the *Gazette* and that, perhaps, he might release him from his obligation not to disclose to Mr Grimsdyke where the diaries were currently being held. With that, the conversation ended in a cordial manner, both men recognising that each must do what the each believed to be right.

'What's all that about, then?' Arkwright demanded of Mr Grimsdyke.

'Well,' Mr Grimsdyke began, 'it would appear that Mr Driglington knows where the diaries are and for that to be so they must have been brought to his personal attention by another of his clients. That means he's either acting for two clients in the same matter – and he's not allowed to do that – or it could be that he's come by some information inadvertently and until be gets that client to release him from his obligation of client confidentiality he just can't say anything. What it boils down to is that our Mr Driglington has got himself into a tight corner and he's going to have to do some quick bobbing and weaving to get himself out of his difficulty.'

'I always said the man was incompetent,' Arkwright said. 'How does a solicitor ever get himself involved with two clients on different sides of the same case?'

'We mustn't judge Mr Driglington too harshly on the bit of information we have,' Mr Grimsdyke told Arkwright. 'All that has to happen is that a prospective client walks into his offices off the street and that person then suddenly shows him the diaries. Mr Driglington can tell that person he cannot act for him but he cannot pass on the information he got from that person in confidence.'

Arkwright understood the thrust of the point being addressed to him, but he did not accept the conclusion which had to be made. 'Ben Driglington knows the diaries are stolen property and that client confidentiality nonsense shouldn't stop him from going to the police. If I go and see Mr Driglington and tell him that I'm going to murder you and I show him the murder weapon, would he regard that as confidential information which hadn't to be passed on to the police?'

'I'm not a lawyer but I think the two cases are different,' said Mr Grimsdyke very hopefully. 'In our case, the theft – if in fact a theft has occurred – has already been committed. In your hypothetical case the crime has yet to be performed. In any event, there's no comparison between murder and theft.'

Arkwright acknowledged that there was a difference in the magnitude of the two offences. However, he was adamant in his view that the theft of the diaries and the theft of a life were both theft and people possessed of knowledge of thefts – actual or proposed – had a duty to report such matters immediately to the police. There was a certain logic in what Arkwright said, for when he asked further whether Mr Driglington would have to report a proposed burglary at Edwin's Emporium to the police, Mr Grimsdyke had to admit it would seem sensible for him to do so even if that information was privileged.

But Mr Grimsdyke knew that matters involving the law were not always settled on a basis of logic.

Mr Grimsdyke was mindful that he had other work to which he had to attend that morning and he drew their philosophical discussions to a close. 'What I've got to do now is to wait until I get a call from Ben Driglington either later today or tomorrow. If he then still refuses to talk to me concerning the whereabouts of the diaries I'll have to talk to people higher up at the bank. But one way or another, this sorry state of affairs has got to be sorted out. I won't be able to discuss with you how the bank is going to act in the affairs of one of its customers, but I do promise that some action will be taken and I'll do my best to keep you informed of developments as far as I am able.'

The two men parted company with Arkwright promising that he'd be back in the bank within two days to see what developments had actually taken place. Mr Grimsdyke was well aware that was both a threat and a promise.

When Arkwright got home he phoned Doris to let her know of the latest turn of events. She told him that she had written to her doctor authorising him to disclose to Mr Grimsdyke that she was barren, and a similar letter had been sent to Mr Grimsdyke giving him permission to approach her doctor to confirm that fact.

Doris asked Arkwright if he would be able to come down to see her again. She was missing him very much and Betty had agreed most willingly to let him stay at her flat whenever he wanted to come to Chiswick. For his part, Arkwright was missing Doris – he was running out of clean clothes to wear. However, he told Doris that he thought he should stay in the Dale until the end of the week to see what action Mr Grimsdyke was going to take to recover the diaries, but he suggested she pencil in a visit from him at the weekend.

Over at the offices of Driglington & Co arrangements were being made to receive the Editor of the *Gazette* and his sidekick. The Editor had already given Seth a puzzled look when he'd mentioned to him that Ben Driglington had told him he hadn't been away from his offices these past few days. The meeting at the solicitor's office was not one to which Seth was looking forward.

Chapter 18

Enter the Police

It came as a considerable relief to Seth Womersley that, when his Editor began to speak to Mr Driglington, no mention was made of his not approaching Driglington & Co when he had been instructed to do so. Instead, the Editor came straight to the point and told Mr Driglington that he'd assumed the payment of a monthly retainer fee was for the sole purpose of retaining the services of his firm for whenever an occasion demanded them. 'If that isn't the case,' the Editor asked, 'then for what purpose is my paper shelling out money each month to Driglington & Co?'

Ben Driglington responded that, *ceteris paribus*, the assumption the Editor had made about the retainer fee was true. However, in this particular instance it wasn't so. 'I'll be happy to advise you,' Mr Driglington said, 'as to how you might dismiss Mr Womersley for lying to you about my being absent from the office last week. However, in the matter of giving an opinion on the publication of Old Tom Bones' diaries I can offer you no advice.'

'I'll be dealing with Mr Womersley personally when we get back to the office,' the Editor replied. 'I take it that I can presume you'll not find yourself in the position of being unable to act for the paper when he contests the presentation I am about to make to him of his P45.' Seth gave a weak and sickly smile.

'You can be quite sure of that,' Mr Driglington promised. 'Now, the problem with the diaries is that they belong to the estate of the late Mr Bones. As far as I can ascertain they were removed from the deceased's house by a person or persons unknown in between the time of Mr Bones' death and the day on which Mr Grimsdyke and I superintended the clearance of the contents of the house. It would therefore seem to me that a theft has occurred, and it is my duty to the deceased's estate to see to the recovery of the late Mr Bones' diaries.

'In one way, you have helped me in that process but, in another, you have created a difficulty. I now know where the diaries are but that information has come to me by way of my meeting with young Mr Womersley who, at that time, was acting on behalf of your paper. The information I possess is therefore privileged and I can't share that knowledge with others without the permission of the paper.

'Should it have happened that somebody on your staff stole the diaries, then, whilst that is a serious matter, I think it can be arranged that no action will be taken against the malefactors if the diaries are delivered up immediately into my possession. However, should this not be the case and you argue that the diaries were acquired in good faith by your paper, then it is almost certain that Mr Grimsdyke at the bank will call in the police to investigate the alleged theft.' The solicitor leant back in his chair and stared at the Editor.

'First of all,' the Editor began, 'nobody at the paper stole the diaries. They came to us from an impeccable source, the name of which I cannot reveal to you. For all you know, the diaries might have been given to us by Old Tom Bones before he died because he thought they might make an interesting column in our paper.'

That was not a thought which had previously occurred to Mr Driglington. It was certainly possible – even if highly unlikely. In any event, if that were to be the case then the Editor would have stated it to be so right at the outset of their discussions together and he would, almost certainly, have been seeking a legal opinion many weeks ago as to what could be published from the diaries.

'Secondly,' continued the Editor, 'the paper has no intention of surrendering the diaries either to you or to Mr Grimsdyke and I expressly forbid you to disclose to him that the diaries are now in the possession of the *Gazette*. I want your assurance that you haven't already told him.'

Mr Driglington went to great pains to emphasise to the Editor that what passed between them in this office was in absolute confidence. However, he did warn the Editor that Mr Grimsdyke was fully aware that he knew where the diaries were because when he'd been directly asked about their location he'd had to reply to Mr Grimsdyke that he could make no answer to his question. The solicitor affirmed to the Editor that if Mr Grimsdyke were able to ascertain that the paper was holding the diaries, then that information would not have come from his lips.

'Well, what do I do now?' the Editor asked Ben Driglington.

'I'm afraid I can't tell you,' Mr Driglington replied. 'I can't advise you further on this matter and I suggest you take the diaries to another solicitor and tell them the whole story.'

'Well, then, can you advise me on this point,' asked the Editor in a sarcastic tone. 'If we pay you to act for us and you don't, then surely we must be entitled to a refund of part of the fees we have paid you?'

'I'll give the matter some thought,' Mr Driglington replied.

'Well, don't charge us for your thoughts,' the Editor responded. 'I'll be sending you a letter with my suggestions.'

Seth and the Editor left the offices of Driglington & Co and made their way back to the *Gazette*. The Editor was not at his most happiest.

'Now, what's all this about you saying that Mr Driglington was away for a few days so that you could go shooting off all of a sudden to London?' the Editor asked Seth.

It was the question Seth had been dreading ever since he'd got back from Chiswick. It was time to come clean and he told the Editor of how he had planned, but had failed, to get an interview with Doris Broughton once his ace investigative techniques had led him to the conclusion that she had gone to stay with Betty Entwistle.

'I suppose I should give you a clout round the ears,' the Editor said. 'I don't like being deceived by a member of my staff, but at least you showed some imagination and initiative. We'll take a rain check on the P45. However, as your punishment you can make that return call we owe Arkwright Broughton – tell him that I'm tied up in meetings and that I've asked you to ring him for me. At least, we know now why he was phoning. If he gives you a roasting for pestering his wife just take what he says on the chin and tell him that you cleared your visit with me before you went swanning off to Chiswick. Tell him that you're sorry if you've upset him and Doris but that you were only trying to do your job. If you butter him up a bit, you'll probably find his bark is far worse than his bite.'

Seth was grateful to the Editor for his support. He'd have been even more grateful if he hadn't lumbered him with having to ring Arkwright. But he consoled himself with the thought it would be like going to visit the dentist – twenty minutes of hell and then it would be all over.

The phone rang in Mr Grimsdyke's office.

'I didn't expect you to get back to me so soon,' he told Ben Driglington.

'I'm afraid it's still no comment,' Mr Driglington announced.

'Can't be helped,' replied Mr Grimsdyke, 'I'll just have to see what the police can find out for me. No doubt in due course they'll be visiting you and you'll also be telling them nothing.'

'That's about the size of it,' Ben Driglington said. 'My lips are sealed. I'll see you in court.'

'I'll ask the judge to see that you get a nice cell,' joked Mr Grimsdyke as he rang off.

Minutes later, Mr Grimsdyke was on the phone to the town's police station.

'Constable Pixter speaking,' said the one in authority.

Mr Grimsdyke introduced himself and briefly explained the facts as he knew them concerning the theft of the diaries. The constable assured Mr Grimsdyke that investigations would be started that very hour.

It was later in the day that Constable Pixter leaned his bicycle against the outer wall of the offices of Driglington & Co. Once inside, the constable asked to see Mr Driglington – but the interview amounted to nothing. There were too many 'no comments' for the liking of Constable Pixter. 'Thank you for your time and cooperation,' he said quite untruthfully to the solicitor as they parted company.

As he unlocked the padlock on his bicycle he noticed Ben Driglington's car parked a sixpenny bus ride away from the kerb.

It mustn't be said that the constable was a vindictive man but as he looked at the car he became especially mindful of his duty towards the community and of the need for its leading citizens to set a good example. It was a simple matter for him to measure the tread on the tyres of the car. No less simple or enjoyable was the second visit to Mr Driglington's to tell him that one tyre was not roadworthy.

It wasn't the cost of a new tyre which caused the solicitor grief but, rather, the inconvenience of having to change to the spare wheel. Within minutes, Fred Dobbs had been promoted from coal merchant to motor mechanic. Fred was not a happy man for the remainder of the day.

By the time Constable Pixter returned to the police station, the sergeant was back at his post. 'Hardly the Great Train Robbery is it?' the sergeant had said on being told of the latest crime on his patch. 'Best get down to the village and make a few enquiries to see what you can find out.'

At the Cat and Fiddle, Mrs Oglethorpe was dishing out the dirt on Doris Broughton. 'She seems to be remarkably well informed about things,' Constable Pixter said to the landlady of the pub.

'Aye, Constable,' she replied, 'she's had a lot to say since Old Tom Bones died and left her nowt in his will.'

Others might have spotted a clue there, but Constable Pixter was not as others might be.

Chapter 19

A Policeman's Lot is not a Happy One

Certainly, Constable Pixter was a methodical man. He took his little black notebook out of his tunic's top pocket and, on a fresh page, wrote down the heading 'Missing Diaries' and the day's date. The first entry read, 'Spoke with landlady of Cat and Fiddle but no relevant information forthcoming.' With that, he put his diary away and buttoned up the pocket of his uniform.

Always visit the scene of the crime was a maxim which had been instilled into him during his basic police training. He was aware that The Limes, where Old Tom Bones had lived out the latter part of his life in the village, had been sold and he was also aware, from what Mr Grimsdyke had told him, that the house had been completely emptied of its possessions. Nevertheless, the constable knew that even bank managers and solicitors did sometimes make mistakes and it could be that both Mr Grimsdyke and Mr Driglington had failed to explore every nook and cranny in that dwelling place. A visit to the house was therefore necessary – even if it were to be as uninformative to him as had been his conversation with the landlady of the Cat and Fiddle. After all, if it were eventually to come to pass that the diaries had been overlooked when the house had been divested of its contents, then he was going to look especially stupid if he had not eliminated the house from the several possible locations where the diaries could be reposing.

The new owners of The Limes were an elderly couple, Mr and Mrs Henry Blenkin, who had moved to the village from Bradford so that they could spend their declining years in the peace and tranquillity of the Dale. They had tended to keep themselves to themselves since taking up residence and, whilst they did attend matins most Sundays at the village church, they had not engaged themselves in other aspects of community life in the village. That this was so was due, in no small measure, to their profound deafness – especially that of Mr Blenkin.

The little black notebook came out again and a new heading made – 'Visit to the Blenkins at The Limes (Old Tom Bones' house as was).' For Constable Pixter it was such a short journey from the Cat and Fiddle to the house that he chose to push his bike there rather than ride it.

It was Mrs Blenkin who eventually opened the door to the policeman. The first series of bangs on the door made by Constable Pixter had gone unheard by the elderly and infirm couple. The constable, having previously ascertained by looking through the lounge window that Mr and Mrs Blenkin were actually in residence, determined that drastic action would need to be taken to attract their attention to his presence at their door. He withdrew his truncheon from his trouser-leg pocket and, verily, he did smite the door with such force that it caused the paint to crack and a dent to appear in the woodwork at the point of impact.

'Who's that tapping on our door?' Mrs Blenkin enquired of her husband.

'What do you say?' he replied – but Mrs Blenkin didn't bother to repeat the question.

It was only the quick reflexes of the constable which saved Mrs Blenkin from suffering a severe blow to her head for, as she opened the door, the policeman's arm and accompanying truncheon were on a downward path towards it.

The vision of a policeman standing on her doorstep was a bad enough sight in itself for Mrs Blenkin who had led a blameless life. But to see him, as she supposed, about to batter her head in caused her such a fright that she immediately fell to the ground in a faint.

Constable Pixter stood as motionless in front of Mrs Mabel Blenkin as she lay motionless in front of him. Women did not usually swoon at the sight of his presence. In fact, none had ever done so before. However, his initial reaction that he had suddenly become an object of female desire was quickly dismissed from his mind as he looked down to his feet where Mrs Blenkin now lay.

Constable Pixter's knowledge of first aid was somewhat limited but he was aware of the recovery position and of the mechanics of administering the kiss of life. He removed his helmet, arranged the seemingly lifeless body of Mrs Blenkin into an appropriate position and placed his mouth against hers.

Now, as well as being deaf, Mr Blenkin was also slightly blind. Not having seen his wife come back from the door he went to investigate what she was up to. The sight he found himself facing was that of his wife lying on the ground and, so it looked very much, being subjected to a serious sexual assault. He picked up the big, heavy stick which was always kept by the door to fend off undesirable callers intruders and, with a force of strength one would not normally

PC Pixter gives kiss of life to Mrs Blenkin

85

associate with a man of his age, he brought the stick down sharply on the head of the stranger at the door.

Constable Pixter immediately joined Mrs Blenkin in a prone position on the doorstep.

The look on the sexual assailant's face suggested he would not be moving of his own accord for a short while, but Mrs Blenkin's face was turning blue.

In a state of some panic, Mr Blenkin made his way back inside his house and went to the telephone. 'Get me the police and an ambulance,' he said to the operator who answered his 999 call. He then made his way to the next door house where Mrs Troughton lived – and who, naturally, had witnessed the entire proceedings from her almost permanent position at her window.

'Very brave of you to knock the policeman out,' she said to Mr Blenkin as she ministered to his wife.

'What did you say?' Mr Blenkin asked.

By the time the ambulance arrived Mrs Blenkin had recovered sufficiently from her ordeal to be able to sit in an upright position. But Constable Pixter, whilst in no mortal danger, continued to lie groaning on the ground.

When the full story of what had happened had been explained to Mrs Blenkin by her neighbour, Mrs Blenkin had replied that she supposed they would look back on the events of that afternoon in the years to come and laugh about them. But there was no smile on the face of Constable Pixter as he was placed on a stretcher and carried to the ambulance to be transported to some distant hospital now that the local health authority had closed down the local cottage hospital.

The police had arrived shortly after the ambulance, and Mrs Blenkin was now perky enough to give her account of what had occurred. 'I just heard this tap on the door,' she said (after the question had been addressed to her three or four times at increasing volumes), 'and as I opened the door there was a great big man in police uniform standing there about to hit me on the head. The next thing I seem to remember was Mrs Troughton here trying to revive me.'

It took many, many, many shouted attempts before Mr Blenkin

was aware that he was being asked to give his account of what had happened.

'I got to the hall to see where Mabel was and I could see the door was open and there she was lying on the ground with that chap gluing himself to her lips. Well, I wasn't going to wait til he'd finished to ask Mabel how it was for her, so I just got my big stick and hit him on the head.'

'Didn't you see he was a policeman?' the officer from the patrol car asked.

'What did you say?' asked Mr Blenkin.

The question was repeated – very loudly.

'No. I didn't know he was a policeman, and if I had I'd have done the same thing,' Mr Blenkin said. 'He's supposed to be keeping people off the streets who attack old, defenceless people – not trying to have his wicked way with them.'

Mr Blenkin then went off on auto pilot about what the world had come to since he was a lad.

'But,' said the patrol car man when he could get a word in, 'Constable Pixter wasn't trying to molest your wife.'

'Who's a pixie?' Mr Blenkin asked.

Fortunately for the officers of the Highway Patrol, Mrs Troughton was able to explain to the officers in precise detail what had actually occurred. 'Through my binoculars,' she said, 'I could even see the hole the officer had made in the door.'

When the cracked paint work on the door and the indentation made by the truncheon were shown to the police officers, they could not help but wonder why Constable Pixter was trying to batter down the door of a harmless old couple. It was not known at the police station that the constable had a propensity for violence – but it was known that if the Richter Scale could be used to register intelligence then a reading for him would be barely discernible.

Cups of tea were made for the Blenkins and they were soon restored to what passed for normality with them. Indeed, as Mrs Blenkin had predicted, they were already beginning to laugh at the temporary upheaval which had occurred in their normal quiet lives.

The police car left and Mrs Troughton once again took up her position in front of the window which overlooked the village. Matters had to be explained to Lucifer who had been abruptly tossed off her lap when she had gone to give aid and succour to Mrs Blenkin. Perhaps it was the bowl of cream which did the trick but – in any event – her cat seemed to be friends with her again.

That evening, the Station Sergeant appeared on the doorstep of the Blenkins with a bouquet of flowers for the lady of the house. It was without question, he explained to them, that the door would be repaired the following day and at no cost to them. Of Constable Pixter, he could only report that he had a large bump on his head and that his return to duties would be dependent on the outcome of a police disciplinary enquiry. 'Even if he is allowed to stay in the force,' the Station Sergeant told them, 'it won't be around here so you needn't worry that you'll meet up with him again.'

The meeting with the Blenkins had taken somewhat longer than the Station Sergeant had envisaged. However, having had to repeat every statement umpteen times had brought him to a greater understanding of the affliction of deafness.

As he was about to leave, he bethought himself to ask about the diaries. Speaking very slowly and very loudly, the Station Sergeant asked the couple if they'd found any of Old Tom Bones' diaries in the house when they'd moved in.

'No,' said Mr Blenkin, 'we don't go to the dairy, the milkman comes here every day.'

'You want a glass of milk?' Mrs Blenkin asked the Station Sergeant.

The easiest course of action was to take the milk – but he'd have preferred something stronger even though he was on duty. The Station Sergeant began again and explained that he'd said 'diaries' and not 'dairies'.

'Oh! Diaries?' Mrs Blenkin said eventually. 'And here I am thinking you were wanting a glass of milk.' She made as if to take the glass away from the Station Sergeant but he indicated – rather than said – he would like to drink it.

'The house was completely empty when we took it over,' Mrs Blenkin said. 'We even looked in the loft to see if any treasure had been left behind but there was only lots of dust.'

By now the excitement of the day had taken its toll on Mr Blenkin.

He was sleeping soundly in his chair. The Station Sergeant picked his way over the outstretched legs and left it to Mrs Blenkin to give her husband his departing good wishes.

The following day, Constable Wellbeloved was put on the trail of the missing diaries.

Chapter 20

The Widow's Window

It was never in the nature of Ben Driglington to turn away a case. Cases meant cash and cash equalled comfort.

The firm of Driglington & Co had seen leadership from five generations of Driglingtons and, when Ben eventually retired and his daughter Sue took over, that would make six generations. Ben was proud of the contribution which he and his forebears had made to the Dale over a hundred years and more, and he only regretted that his only child was a daughter and not a son.

One day, Sue would marry and her name would change. Should, perchance, one of her offspring become a solicitor then that child would join the firm but would not carry to the firm the family name of Driglington – not unless, if by some happy chance, Sue married a Driglington. That possibility was ever-present in the mind of Ben. Whenever he chanced to meet a person bearing his family name he was never backwards in coming forwards to ask if that person had a son who, on close inspection, might measure up to his ideal of a husband for his daughter, Sue.

Ben Driglington, Arkwright and Doris Broughton and Edwin Pickles were all much of an age. At school it was Ben who had been considered to be the one with the brains and it was he, alone, who had won a scholarship to the County Grammar School and, from there, had gone on to read law at Durham University. Arkwright, Edwin and Doris had all withered on the academic vine and had left school at the earliest opportunity. But, for all his scholarly learning at Grammar School and University, Ben Driglington's education was not complete, for the opportunity had never presented itself for him to attend little Bessie Sidebottom's special biology lessons. A virgin he entered the educational system, and a virgin he left it, albeit with the degree of Bachelor of Laws.

After University, Ben Driglington returned to the small Dale's town out of which the family law firm practised. He duly completed his articles under his father's benign care and influence and, in the fullness of time, he was admitted to the Roll of Solicitors and became a junior partner in the family firm. Yet still he was a virgin.

Josiah Thomas Arkwright Ellington Driglington, the name of Ben's father when it was writ in full, took a stern view of life. He was rich, could afford anything, lived in a grand style in a grand house and had servants aplenty. But in his son he had imbued the virtue of unbridled thrift. On matters of a sexual nature he was Victorian in outlook.

It was shortly after Ben had become a junior partner that his father had taken him on one side and asked if he were still a virgin. Blushing profusely, Ben had to admit to his father that he was still in a state of innocence.

The father shook his head in disbelief and asked his son whether he believed in sex before marriage.

Now, at that time, Ben believed he was something of a wit and had replied, 'Not if it holds up the wedding service.' Josiah regarded the answer as flippant and was not amused.

'In our society,' Josiah counselled his son, 'we marry to unite similar houses together. Sex is a secondary matter. If it happens when a union takes place that there is a coincidence of wants and needs in that area of a marriage, then it is fortunate and perhaps exceptional. People of our class, both satisfied and unsatisfied in holy wedlock, have the ancient privilege of taking our pleasure with the lower classes as and when we feel there is a need to be met.'

The matter was not discussed further but Ben assumed – after all he did have a university degree – that the homily he had received from his father was, in fact, an instruction. Ben therefore set about satisfying this particular pleasure. He considered carefully those members of the working class who were known to him and who, he believed, would either regard it as an honour to be deflowered by him or take it as a compliment that he would wish to follow where others had who'd gone before him. Thus it was that, rather belatedly in life, Ben Driglington had his innocence stripped away.

It was some months later that Ben became acquainted with the significance of 'missing a period'. At first he was astounded that the lack of a full stop could cause such anguish to a member of the illiterate working class – and to a woman member at that. Until it had been explained to him, he had not envisaged that a meeting of seminal fluids would have such a dire consequence as that now being addressed at him. In desperation, he turned to his father for advice and was given an assurance that matters would be taken care of. Quite what his father meant by those words was something Ben thought it prudent not to enquire into too closely. Suffice it to say the incident was not referred to again and the 'lady' in question set at rest the claims she had been pressing against Ben. But, as we are all aware, all chickens eventually come home to roost.

Nobody lives for ever and, when, in due course, Josiah Thomas Arkwright Ellington Driglington joined the heavenly throng, Ben became the senior partner of Driglington & Co. Elevated to that lofty position, he decided that the time had come for him to be joined in holy wedlock. The lucky lady was The Honourable Margaret Ponsonby, daughter of the Lord Farnley.

The marriage was not a success. Whereas The Honourable Margaret enjoyed nothing more than a good spend and expensive trips to London, the accumulation and retention of wealth meant everything to Ben Driglington. His frugal attitude to life was due to the ways instilled into him by his father. Try as she did, the Honourable Margaret could not bring her husband to an amendment of life. An amicable parting of the ways between the two of them was arranged.

Work was the force which drove Ben Driglington and now, with no wife at hand but with a bairn to support and raise on his own, he never lost an opportunity to take on a new client and never lost a client once in his legal embrace.

It was therefore a matter of much disappointment to Ben Driglington that he was not now in a position to advise the *Gazette* on the publication of Old Tom Bones' diaries. The fact that the paper was going to have to give instructions to another solicitor represented a loss of income for him and his firm. Even worse, he feared that once the *Gazette* was in the clutches of a different legal adviser then he might lose their patronage completely. The point had not been lost on him that the Editor had been more than slightly miffed that the retainer fee they had been paying him for so many years seemed to account for nothing when they had a real need of him and his legal expertise.

Whilst it went against the grain he had, reluctantly, come to the conclusion that if he were to retain the *Gazette* in his client base then he would have to show a degree of magnanimity towards them. The manifestation of his generosity would be by way of a refund of some of the retainer fees they had paid to his firm. However, corresponding measures would have to be made to reduce operating costs of Driglington & Co until the refund had been recouped.

No less painful for Ben Driglington was the fact that he could no longer act for the bank in the matter of the winding-up of the estate of the late Old Tom Bones. To lose two clients in one day was a matter of great sadness to Ben Driglington – almost an act of negligence.

As the *Gazette* would not free him from his obligation not to disclose his knowledge of the whereabouts of the diaries to Mr Grimsdyke, he was left with two choices. First, he could simply choose to go to the court himself, present the facts of the case to a judge and ask to be released from his bond of secrecy to the *Gazette*. To do so, though, would do little for his diminishing credibility at the *Gazette*, the editor of which might well see such action as treacherous and traitorous.

Or, the alternative course of action would be just to sit back and allow the police investigations set in hand by Mr Grimsdyke to run their course. If those investigations proved to be successful, then it would be through no fault of his that the paper was exposed as being the current possessors of the diaries.

But another possibility could occur. Mr Grimsdyke might, on behalf of the estate he was responsible for winding up, go directly to the court and demand that he disclose the information he was concealing. Whilst that might be embarrassing for him he could, at least, plead with the Editor of the *Gazette* that he'd had to do as the court directed him. However, knowing that papers can sniff out a good story when they see one, the Editor might suggest to him that he stand firm and refuse to comply with the decision of the judge. The paper could then portray him as a martyr whilst he languished in jail.

The idea of being inconvenienced by a spell in the pokey hole until he repented of his contempt of court was not one which held any attraction to Ben Driglington. From his work as a prosecuting solicitor he had seen the type of people who comprised the prison community, and they were not people with whom, to coin a phrase, he would wish to spend time.

On careful consideration and after discussions with his daughter, Sue, he decided to sit tight and await what emerged from the police enquiries into the theft of the diaries.

PC Wellbeloved was a man of different character from Constable Pixter. Not only did he possess a university degree but he also held a handful of diplomas ranging from Food Hygiene to a Licentiateship of the Royal Academy of Music. But that was not the only difference between those two officers of the law. Whereas Constable Pixter had possessed a pedal cycle, PC Wellbeloved was the proud owner of a lightly powered motor scooter.

His first visit to the village was – as had been Constable Pixter's – to the Cat and Fiddle. He came in for a certain amount of ribbing from the regulars who, by now, all knew of Constable Pixter's fiasco at the home of the Blenkins. 'Who are you going to beat up today?' he'd been asked so many times that the joke was beginning to wear rather thin. Nevertheless, PC Wellbeloved took the teasing of him in a good spirit and, for their part, the villagers thought he was a good sport and accepted him as a friend.

The landlady offered him a pint – 'Provided he could give her an assurance that it wouldn't turn him violent.' The policeman took the drink and, having drained the glass, whipped out his truncheon. The landlady blanched. 'Only joking!' said PC Wellbeloved returning the truncheon to its home. The joke on the landlady went down well with the regulars. And when she had recovered from the shock she, too, laughed.

'What are you doing in the village?' the landlady asked.

'Well,' replied PC Wellbeloved, 'it appears that Old Tom Bones was very careful to keep a diary of everything that went on in his life and all of his diaries have gone missing. I'm here to try and find them. I suppose that Constable Pixter thought they might still be at the house where Old Tom lived but I gather they weren't.'

'Yes,' replied the landlady, 'Old Tom was very particular about writing up his diaries. He often used to bring one in here of an evening and read out to us what happened ten or even twenty plus years ago. In fact, he treated us to one of his gems only the night before he died.'

'I don't suppose that any of you have seen the diaries since he died, have you?' PC Wellbeloved asked as he turned to face the locals. But nobody had.

'Was the house broken into?' Albert Boot, the village newsagent asked.

'We never had any report to that effect,' the police officer replied.

'You could go and see Mrs Troughton who lives next door to Old Tom's House,' Albert said. 'Mind you, she'll see you before you see her. She doesn't miss a trick looking out of that front room window of hers.'

PC Wellbeloved thanked Albert Boot for his information and *phut phutted* on his scooter over to where Mrs Troughton lived. Before he was half way up her garden path Mrs Troughton was standing at her opened door.

'Come in, officer,' she said.

PC Wellbeloved liked being called 'officer'. For a period, he'd served in the army and had risen to the exalted rank of Lance Corporal in the Military Police. He had tried for a commission – he'd always wanted pips on his shoulders – but had failed. Now, being called 'officer' was some compensation for that disappointment.

'There's a slight problem,' he told Mrs Troughton. 'Old Tom Bones' diaries have been stolen from his house, but there's never been any evidence of a burglary having taken place. I don't suppose that you ever saw anything odd going on at his house after he'd died, did you?'

'I sit here at my window from morning to night, and I can tell you that I've seen lots of odd things going on. I bet Bill Merryweather doesn't know what his wife Beryl gets up to after he's gone to work. But I've never seen anything odd at Old Tom's house. He was such a nice old man. Did you ever know him?' Mrs Troughton asked.

PC Wellbeloved had to confess that he'd never had the pleasure of meeting Old Tom as, until only the day before, he'd been stationed in the neighbouring Dale. However, he had heard of him as he had heard tell of all the other colourful characters in the Dale. Whilst he would have been interested to hear of Mrs Merryweather's antics, he was not visiting Mrs Troughton to become acquainted with that type of gossip – leastwise, not that day. He turned the conversation back to Old Tom's house.

'Did Old Tom ever have any visitors?' he asked.

'Nobody ever, ever called on Old Tom at his house except for Mrs Oglethorpe,' Mrs Troughton said. 'I can tell you she was more than a bit put out when she found out that he'd not left her anything in his will and that he'd left everything to that nice Doris Broughton.' Covering Lucifer's ears, she asked if he knew whether it was true that Doris really was the mother of Old Tom's child.

'It's not for me to speculate on that,' PC Wellbeloved replied. 'How often did Mrs Oglethorpe go to Old Tom's House?' he asked.

'Every day at ten sharp,' Mrs Troughton said. 'She were never a minute late or a minute early. Since Old Tom died she's only been there once and that was on the day his will was published in the paper. She has her paper delivered – I see the lad take it to her house every day. It was about two minutes after that she went over to the house carrying a suitcase. I couldn't help but notice that it looked a deal fuller and heavier when she came out than it had when she'd gone in. And do you know she had the same suitcase with her when that young reporter from the *Gazette* came to pick her up in his car. I thought she were going on a holiday somewhere but she came back with him about an hour later and it was clear that her suitcase was now empty.'

'That's very helpful, Mrs Troughton,' the policeman told her. 'I think I'll pay Mrs Oglethorpe a visit.'

Mrs Troughton did her best to get PC Wellbeloved to stay and have a cup of tea with her. 'It gets very lonely here on my own since my husband Bert passed on. Lucifer is good company but it's not the same as entertaining a young man to tea.'

PC Wellbeloved said that he was very sorry that he would have to decline her kind offer of hospitality but he did promise Mrs Troughton that he would return another day for cakes and a chat.

'It's no use your going to see Mrs Oglethorpe now,' Mrs Troughton said. 'She'll be at the village whist drive and won't be back for another half hour.'

'Well,' replied PC Wellbeloved, 'perhaps I can trespass on your good nature and have the tea and cakes I so ungenerously declined a few minutes ago?' And a right good tea it was.

As predicted, Mrs Oglethorpe was back at her house half an hour later. She was about to receive an unwelcome visit.

Chapter 21

Taken Prisoner

PC Wellbeloved gave Alice Oglethorpe time enough to get her coat off before he went over to her house.

She was somewhat taken aback when, on opening her front door, she found an officer of the law standing on the threshold.

'Yes?' snapped Alice. 'State your business and be on your way.'

PC Wellbeloved had not warmed to Alice Oglethorpe from what Mrs Troughton had to tell him about her. Seeing her in the flesh confirmed all that had been confided in him by the Lady of the Window.

'There's a matter I would like to talk to you about, and it might be best if we could go inside rather than have our discussion on the doorstep,' PC Wellbeloved began.

'We can talk here on the doorstep, young man,' Mrs Oglethorpe replied tartly. 'I don't invite tradesmen and the likes of you into my house.'

'I don't think that's a very helpful attitude,' PC Wellbeloved said. 'Now we can either go inside your home and talk civilly, or I can take you down to the police station and we can conduct the interview there.'

Whilst PC Wellbeloved was courteous in his manner of address, there was a definite firmness and timbre of steel in the tone of his voice. Alice Oglethorpe did not particularly relish the idea of a ride on the back of PC Wellbeloved's scooter, and she did not think, if push came to shove, that he would actually force her to ride with him back to the station sitting on the rear seat of his mechanically propelled velocipede. She thought she'd call his bluff.

'No. You're going to talk to me here on the doorstep or not at all, or I'm going back indoors,' she said, arms firmly positioned on her hips and her thin lips set firm on her harsh face. After a pause she made as if to go inside her house.

'As you wish,' PC Wellbeloved replied. He was watched by Mrs Oglethorpe as he walked back up the garden path to the road where he had parked his scooter and, on his radio, called up the Station Sergeant to appraise him of the situation.

Mrs Oglethorpe had never previously been in trouble with the police but she was generally held to be a 'nasty piece of work' by all who knew her. The Station Sergeant had once had an altercation with her in a private capacity at one of the Dale's flower shows. She had deliberately – but it couldn't be proved beyond peradventure – knocked his almost certain-to-win prize tomatoes onto the floor of the marquee and then squashed them with her foot prior to the judging taking pace. In the event it was her tomatoes which won the prize for 'best in show'.

'I think it's about time that Mrs High and Mighty took a tumble from her perch,' the Station Sergeant told PC Wellbeloved. 'Bring her in for questioning.'

Now it happened it was court day on the morrow and those about to be tried before the justices occupied almost all the police cells. Some of the alleged offenders would, the next day, find themselves back in the bosom of their respective families whilst others would be off to residential accommodation at Northallerton where it pleased Her Majesty to house some of her delinquent subjects. Thus, by happy chance, a Black Maria was currently parked in the police station yard.

'We'll bring her here in the mobile prison – that'll wipe the nasty sneer off her face,' said the Station Sergeant.

PC Wellbeloved walked back down the garden path to the front door from where Mrs Oglethorpe was still standing and glowering at him.

'I'm going to have to ask you to accompany me to the station,' he told Mrs Oglethorpe.

'You needn't think I'm going with you on the back of that

contraption,' she said, pointing to his scooter. 'And I'm certainly not going to walk to the station.'

'I wouldn't dream of offering you either of those two possibilities,' PC Wellbeloved said. 'Transport appropriate to the situation will be here in ten minutes. I suggest you go inside and put your coat on so that you'll be ready for when the van arrives.'

PC Wellbeloved watched with interest the reaction on Mrs Oglethorpe's face. Already red, it was now turning crimson.

Mrs Oglethorpe had seen the local police vans, the back parts of which always seemed to accommodate smelly police dogs. 'And you needn't think I'm going in the back of one of your stinking vans,' she said. 'You can send for one of your cars.'

'I think you'll find the vehicular transport which has been arranged for you will be more than satisfactory,' PC Wellbeloved replied.

It caused something of a stir in the village when the Black Maria arrived and stopped outside the house of Mrs Oglethorpe. The sight of two burly policemen bearing down on Mrs Oglethorpe as she continued to stand defiantly and impudently on her doorstep only served to add extra drama to the occasion.

'I think,' said PC Wellbeloved to Mrs Oglethorpe in his best pantomime voice, 'that your carriage awaits. Lock your door and go off with my two colleagues.'

Mrs Oglethorpe stood her ground. As the two officers approached her she clenched her fist and gave one of them a blooded nose. A short, sharp kick on the shins was directed accurately at the other officer. But, fast as she was in resisting detention, she was no match for PC Wellbeloved who had her arms pinned behind her back before she could inflict further damage on the brave men of the North Riding Constabulary. The handcuffs were slipped onto her wrists and she was cautioned and arrested for assaulting two police officers before she'd had time to draw breath.

'Albert,' said Nellie Wainwright, who'd just arrived on the scene, 'what's going on over there?'

Since his trip to Belgium earlier in the week, Albert Boot had put it about that he no longer wished to have his name pronounced 'Albert', but *Al-bare* – which he considered to be much more dignified and less open to being shortened to the rather common form of 'Bert'.

'It's *Al-bare*,' he gently reminded Mrs Wainwright. 'The police came to arrest Alice Oglethorpe and she assaulted two of them. And then that copper with the Noddy bike handcuffed her right smartish and then bundled her into that police van.'

The voice of Alice Oglethorpe could be heard above the noise of the van's engine as it drove off to the police station. Nobody in the village had ever witnessed such proceedings before. It was the talk of the snug at the Cat and Fiddle that night.

'Makes a change hearing people talk about Alice Oglethorpe rather than her talking about other people,' the landlady said. 'I wonder what it was she's done to get carted off like that by the police?'

'Perhaps they thought she'd taken the diaries of Old Tom Bones,' said little Bessie Sidebottom who liked to sink a pint or two with the men in the saloon bar of an evening. 'I'd like to see those coppers mess me around like they did Alice Oglethorpe,' little Bessie said more in hope than expectation.

The circumstances surrounding the arrest had been radioed through to the Station Sergeant. By the time the van arrived, Alice Oglethorpe had quietened down and the penny was beginning to drop with her that perhaps she had acted too hastily in refusing to answer the questions of PC Wellbeloved in the comfort of her own home.

'Put her in cell nine,' the Station Sergeant ordered once she was out of the van. 'We'll deal with her after she's had a bit of time to cool down.'

'I want to see my solicitor,' Alice Oglethorpe demanded. 'Get me Mr Driglington.'

'All in good time,' the Station Sergeant assured her. And with that, Alice Oglethorpe was frogmarched into her cell. The heavy door shut with a loud bang and the strange sound of hearing the key turn in the lock brought her, for the first time, to a full realisation of her parlous predicament.

Half an hour later a very subdued Alice Oglethorpe was taken from her cell to an interview room. WPC Mavis Posselthwaite stood in attendance as PC Wellbeloved began his questioning.

'What were you doing at Old Tom Bones' house on the morning you had read about his will in the *Gazette*?' he asked.

'I didn't go to his house that day,' Alice Oglethorpe replied. 'And I want to see my solicitor.'

'All in good time,' PC Wellbeloved told her.

'The last time I was at Old Tom's house was the day after he'd died and after he'd been taken off to the funeral parlour. I only went to collect my apron and a few other odds and ends of mine which I kept at his house whilst I was his cleaner. And then I came home,' she said.

'Oh,' she added, 'I did empty his rubbish bins and put the black sacks out for the dustman to collect, but I didn't do my normal cleaning because I didn't know whether I'd be paid for it. If I was going to steal anything of Old Tom's I'd have done it then.'

'The point is,' PC Wellbeloved observed, 'that at that time you didn't know Old Tom had not included you in his Will. You couldn't steal anything then because you might have been stealing something which had been left to you. What's more, we've got a witness who says you were seen leaving Old Tom Bones' house on the day his Will was published in the *Gazette*.'

'I'm not saying anything more until I've spoken to Mr Driglington. I've seen it on the telly – I've got a right to make a telephone call and I want to do that right now,' said Mrs Oglethorpe. With that, she just sat back in her chair, folded her arms in front of her chest and buttoned up her lips.

PC Wellbeloved left the interview room to contact Mr Driglington – who never lost an opportunity to add a new client to his list.

'What's her problem?' Ben Driglington asked the officer.

'Assaulting two policemen. I think it's best that you come down here as soon as possible and have a quiet chat with her,' PC Wellbeloved replied.

It was about forty minutes later that Ben Driglington arrived at the police station. In the interval, Alice Oglethorpe had been returned to her cell.

Ben Driglington was shown the charge sheet and he asked to have a conference with his client in private. He was aware of who Alice Oglethorpe was and he did not like her but it was going to be for him to say for her in court what she would say for herself had she the ability to do so. 'Why was she being arrested?' Mr Driglington asked as he was led into Alice Oglethorpe's cell.

'She was being brought in for questioning about the theft of Old Tom Bones' diaries. When asked to assist us in our enquiries she became violent,' PC Wellbeloved explained.

By now, Ben Driglington was in the cell and facing Mrs Oglethorpe. PC Wellbeloved said he would leave them together but that he would have to lock the cell door. He told Mr Driglington to bang on the door when his interview was over and he wished to come out.

Ben Driglington began his interview with a terrible sinking feeling in his stomach. He could now guess that Mrs Oglethorpe was the 'impeccable source' from which the *Gazette* had obtained Old Tom Bones' diaries. He also guessed that Mrs Oglethorpe had not come by the diaries in a legitimate way, which would make her guilty of theft – and that would put the *Gazette* in a difficult position if Mrs Oglethorpe were to be convicted in due course. But what was even worse was that he could not take on Mrs Oglethorpe as his client because of his now ever increasing conflicts of interest over the diaries. 'Is there nobody,' he said to himself, 'who wants my services who is not involved in these damn diaries?'

'Can you tell me what happened earlier today?' he asked Mrs Oglethorpe.

'I'd just got home from playing whist in the village hall,' Mrs Oglethorpe began, 'when there was a knock on my door, and there was this young policeman standing there. He wanted to come into my house but I didn't see why he couldn't discuss his business with me on the doorstep and I told him so. He got stroppy and said that if he couldn't come in then he'd force me to go to the police station with him. Then this police van arrived and two big coppers got hold of me and roughed me up so I punched one on the nose and kicked the other on the shin. They didn't like that and then the first policeman forced my arms up really high behind my back which really hurt and he then put some handcuffs on me. Then they brought me here. I want all of those policemen arrested for assaulting me.'

Ben Driglington didn't say anything. This was her side of the

103

story and it was his experience gained over many years that those who had been forcibly arrested often gave a not entirely factual account of the facts surrounding their arrest. At worst, as often as not, it was six of one and half a dozen of the other when it came to determining the actual facts of the case.

Eventually Ben Driglington spoke. 'What was it that the police were wanting to question you about?' Ben asked.

'Well,' Alice Oglethorpe said, 'it seems they think I stole Old Tom Bones' diaries.'

Mr Driglington put the cap back on his fountain pen, gathered together his papers and stood up. 'I'm very sorry, Mrs Oglethorpe,' he said, 'but I cannot represent you in this matter because it presents me with a conflict of interest with two others who are already my clients. One of these is the late Mr Tom Bones, and the other is someone whose name I am not at liberty to reveal to you. I can only suggest to you that you ask PC Wellbeloved to provide you with a list of solicitors and that you select one from that list. I am quite confident that any one of them will be able to give you all the advice you need. They will also be able to represent you in court on the assault charge and, should it come to pass, the charge of the theft of the diaries of the late Old Tom Bones.'

With that he shook hands with Mrs Oglethorpe and knocked on the cell door. PC Wellbeloved appeared almost immediately.

Once outside the cell, Mr Driglington explained, without going into detail, that he was unable to represent Mrs Oglethorpe. He asked that she be given the list of solicitors so that she could choose a new lawyer to represent her.

It was about three hours later that Mr Curtis of Evershaw and Curtis arrived to see the now stricken Mrs Oglethorpe. Sitting alone together in the interview room of the police station he asked Mrs Oglethorpe to describe the events leading up to her arrest. This time she gave a more faithful rendition of what had actually happened earlier that day at her house, and she conceded that she had been less than helpful to PC Wellbeloved. Having heard her statement Mr Curtis told her it would be his advice that she should plead guilty to the assault charge when she appeared before the magistrates the next day. 'Knowing what your village is like,' he said, 'I imagine there will be not a few of the villagers who can attest to the case which the police will put forward.' Alice indicated that she agreed with his advice.

'Now, what's all this about some diaries?' he asked. 'Did you steal them?' But before she had chance to reply, he advised Mrs Oglethorpe that, although any charge involving the theft of the diaries would not be dealt with by the court the following day, it was clearly an offence which police were going to investigate thoroughly. 'You must know,' he said, 'that in due course they will be back to question you further, and they'll probably start asking you questions about the diaries again tonight.'

Mr Curtis took out his pipe and lit it. He did not intend it to be a question when he asked Alice Oglethorpe if she minded if he smoked.

'If you did steal the diaries then it will go better for you if you hand them over now,' Mr Curtis advised.

This put Alice Oglethorpe on the spot. She didn't want to admit to stealing the diaries, and still less did she want to say that she had sold them on to the *Gazette*.

Mr Curtis could see her reluctance to answer. 'You must trust me,' he told her. 'I'm here to advise you as to what is in your best interests. It's then up to you to decide whether you want to take my advice, because I shall follow your instructions if a case is ever brought against you in the courts.'

Alice Oglethorpe thought long and hard before replying.

'I didn't actually steal them,' she began. And she then told Mr Curtis of how, quite by chance, she had read one of the diaries during the course of performing her domestic duties at Old Tom Bones' house.

'I knew if the diaries got into the wrong hands after Old Tom had died,' she said, 'then it could be quite embarrassing for a number of folk in the village. I only took them from the house for safe keeping and I was going to burn them after all the fuss and bother had died down about Doris Broughton getting all of Old Tom's money because she'd had his baby.'

'So you've told nobody that you've got the diaries, and you haven't revealed to anybody anything you've read in them?' Mr Curtis asked.

Now Alice Oglethorpe recognised that when the *Gazette* started publication of the diaries, it would be clear that the gossip she had been generating could only have come from her having read the diaries.

'Well,' she said, 'I suppose I've let the odd snippet of information slip out in the village in the past week or so.'

'That's not too good,' her solicitor told her. 'But if you were to hand over the diaries now I imagine we could come to some deal with the police. However, I have to say that from what you've already told me, a charge of theft will almost certainly be brought against you. If only you hadn't talked about what you'd read it would have been that much simpler to defend you. I don't think there's much doubt that the police will be able to produce witnesses to establish that you must have read and talked about what's in these diaries. But things could be worse. You could have passed the diaries on to another person or, even worse, sold them to the *News of the World*.'

Poor Alice Oglethorpe! Matters were not just going from bad to worse, but from calamity to downright disaster.

'I've not got the diaries any more,' she told Mr Curtis.

'Do you mean that you did burn them then?' Mr Curtis asked.

'No,' she replied. 'I gave them to the *Gazette*.'

'Let's be precise about this,' Mr Curtis demanded. 'Gave or sold?'

'I'm afraid I sold them,' Alice Oglethorpe replied and promptly burst into tears.

'I think we've got a rather serious situation on our hands,' Mr Curtis said as he relit his pipe. 'With luck, because you have no criminal record you might get away with a caution and being bound over to keep the peace for your assault. More probably, you will get a suspended sentence – kicking a policeman, let alone thumping one on the nose, is more serious than doing something similar to your next door neighbour. Let's be thankful the police didn't have a dog with them so you didn't have the chance to kick that as well. Magistrates are very hot on cruelty to dogs these days.' He lit his pipe yet again.

'Now with regards to the theft of the diaries, if you admit to that offence now, the magistrates might be persuaded to take a more lenient view than if you are brought before them at a later date to face that charge. And I have to advise you that it's highly likely from what you have already told me that is an almost certain outcome to these events. If that were to happen, and if you were given a suspended sentence for the assault then you will not only be sentenced for the theft but an additional and stiffer sentence could be imposed for the assault. A term in jail is a distinct possibility if the two offences are not dealt with together. And it cannot be guaranteed that you will not go to jail for the theft quite irrespective of the assault charge against you.'

By now, Alice Oglethorpe was shaking. The prospect of having to spend that night in a police cell was bad enough – but to be incarcerated in a jail for even a few months filled her with dread. 'What do you advise me to do?' she asked Mr Curtis.

'On what the evidence against you looks likely to be, I would advise you to plead guilty to the assault and to start talking to the police now about the theft. If you admit that second offence we can ask the police to deal with them both together. They won't have time to prepare the case for the theft by tomorrow morning, but I'll suggest to them that, in view of your remorse for the assault and for your promised cooperation in the matter of the theft, you should be allowed to go home tonight. With our joint assurance that you will appear before the magistrates tomorrow morning, I think I shall be able to persuade the police to ask the magistrates to suspend their hearing of your charges on both counts to a later date.'

'If that's your advice, then I'll take it,' Alice Oglethorpe replied. 'You know far more about matters like this than I do. Do you really think they'll let me go home tonight?'

'We can but try,' replied Mr Curtis.

Mr Curtis left the interview room and sought out PC Wellbeloved, now on overtime. An hour later, Mrs Oglethorpe was on her way back home in Mr Curtis' car. He promised to collect her at nine the following morning.

It had been, as she put it later, 'a bugger of a day' for her and, what's more, when she got into her house she found she'd had a visit from burglars in her absence. Perhaps it was poetic justice, but the Judas money she'd received from the *Gazette* for the diaries had all been stolen.

Chapter 22

A Day in Court

It was a bright day. Alice Oglethorpe got out of bed; not that she'd had much sleep that night.

After washing and dressing she didn't feel much like breakfast, but she was mindful of the fact that this might be the last opportunity for her to eat in her own home for a few months if the worst of Mr Curtis' predictions came to pass. She put two slices of bread in the toaster and made herself a cup of coffee.

When the bread was toasted she found that she couldn't face them. She tore the slices of toast into little pieces, opened her kitchen window and threw them out for the birds. The cup of coffee – and three others after that – were, however, drunk. Another hour would have to pass before Mr Curtis called to take her to court. It would be a long hour.

Over at The Grange, Mrs Christina Gibbs JP was preparing herself for her day in court. It had been a latent social conscience which had occasioned her to offer her services to the magistracy some thirty years ago and now, today, she was one of the Chairmen of the Bench for Widdledale.

Sitting in court with her this morning would be Mrs Helen Pye JP – a married mother with four children. Mrs Pye was not one to suffer fools too gladly (or even at all) and, given the chance, would have had the village stocks brought back into regular use. On one occasion when a malcontent in the dock was being particularly obstructive in the answering of questions addressed to him, she had been heard to utter to the then Chairman of the Bench that if she could have half an hour with the miserable creature and the use of a ducking stool then she would soon change his attitude to the proceedings of the court. And it was on more than one occasion she'd been told of the inappropriateness of the tee shirt she'd taken to wearing whilst sitting on the bench which carried the slogan 'Hang the Bastards High'.

After receiving a letter from the Lord Chancellor on the matter of her dress in the *execution* (Mrs Pye liked that word) of her court work, she had taken the hint and dressed herself more soberly.

Prior to moving to the Dale, Mrs Pye had been a Justice of the Peace in Scarborough. At one trial, a solicitor had asked a witness – who happened to be a trawler man – whether a certain event had surprised him. 'Surprised,' the witness had replied, 'you could have buggered me through my oil skins.' The puzzled look which had then come across the face of the Chairman of the Bench was only lifted when Mrs Pye had explained to the Chairman that the witness was trying to say that *he'd been taken aback*. Well informed on the seamier side of life, Mrs Pye would often be an ideal antidote to Mrs Gibbs who rarely saw issues in terms of black and white and who was, some said, a little too keen on protecting the interests of the offenders rather then the victims.

Also sitting on the Bench that day would be Colonel Sir Willoughby Forsythe-Bramley, DSO, MC, TD, JP – one of whose ancestors had raised a regiment in the Dales for the Cavaliers. It had been his ancestor's misfortune to be on the losing side of his first battle with the Roundheads and, for all the trouble he'd taken for King and Country, had ended up with having his head chopped off.

Sir Willoughby was a great believer in boot camps for juvenile offenders or, alternatively, deportation to Wales – a place he held to be not so much a country but, more, a bloody good place to put a reservoir.

Christina Gibbs was going to have her hands full reigning in on the excesses of her fellow magistrates that day – perhaps more so than with the committed excesses of the citizenry who would be facing her from the dock.

At the appointed hour the three magistrates filed into the court

109

amidst the general shuffling of feet as those assembled before them rose to their feet.

The first case was a simple one of a man using offensive language in the street. All went well until a nervous policeman giving evidence for the first time in court was asked by Mrs Gibbs what the man was alleged to have said. 'He called me a *worship*, you bastard,' he said. A smile crossed the face of the prisoner at the bar and Sir Willoughby turned puce. It was only Mrs Pye who actually laughed out loud.

The second case was also not without incident. Billy Rowntree had an aversion to paying what he considered to be exorbitant prices for spirits at the pub or at the off-licence counter at Edwin Pickles' Emporium. Accordingly, he had hit upon the expedient device of distilling his own nettle wine, the proof of which was somewhat in excess of that of a good bottle of gin. He was facing a charge of being in possession of an illicit still. Whilst he admitted possessing such a piece of equipment, it was his defence that he had never used it. The evidence against Billy Rowntree – namely the still itself – was produced in court for the magistrates to see and proceedings were delayed temporarily as Sir Willoughby made some hurried sketches of the equipment. On being asked by Mrs Gibbs as to whether he had anything to say before being sentenced, Billy Rowntree stated that he wished a number of other offences to be taken into account. Mrs Gibbs raised an eyebrow and enquired what those might be. Mr Rowntree replied that the first which came to his mind, was rape, because as it was possession that seemed to be the offence, he had to confess he had the equipment but (like his still) he'd never used it for that purpose.

Mrs Gibbs was not impressed by the logic of his argument and before he could site other examples an order was passed down from the Bench for the still to be confiscated and for Billy Rowntree to pay a fine.

And now it was the turn of Mrs Oglethorpe to appear before the Bench. She stood in the dock, a diminutive figure as terrified as if she were meeting her Maker on the Day of Judgement. Mr Curtis gave her a reassuring glance and a half smile from the defence bench but it did not afford Mrs Oglethorpe much comfort.

The charge of assault against the two policemen was read out and she was asked how she wished to plead. 'Guilty,' she said, her voice quaking with emotion and tears beginning to form in her eyes.

Now, Sir Willoughby was also a member of the County Police Authority and he took none too kindly to one of his lads being beaten up by a seemingly frail woman. He glowered at Mrs Oglethorpe.

Perhaps it was only in her confused imagination, but she could have sworn that he ran his fingers across his throat as he pretended to adjust his tie. At the same time, Mrs Pye rummaged in her handbag and, temporarily, placed her black handkerchief on her head until she had come across her cough drops.

'May it please your Worships,' PC Wellbeloved began, 'there is a further offence which Mrs Oglethorpe would like to be brought before the court which the police are currently investigating, concerning the theft of a number of diaries belonging to the late Mr Thomas Bones. We would ask Your Worships that this case of assault be deferred until we are in a position to bring both charges against Mrs Oglethorpe before you'

Mrs Oglethorpe in Court

111

Mrs Gibbs then asked Mrs Oglethorpe if she had any objections to that proposed course of action. It was Mr Curtis who replied for her, stating that his client would be pleading guilty to both charges and would be cooperating fully with the police in their on-going enquiries into the theft of the diaries. In the light of this statement, he asked if the magistrates would consider releasing Mrs Oglethorpe from custody. He pointed out that she was full of regret for her action in assaulting the two policemen and that she was unlikely to pose a threat to the community at any time in the future.

Mrs Gibbs thanked Mr Curtis for his contribution and consulted with her colleagues. From her initial exchanges with Sir Willoughby and Mrs Pye, she quickly came to the conclusion that they should retire to their anteroom where they could discuss their decision without the presence of an audience.

In the privacy of their room, Sir Willoughby expressed the view that Mrs Oglethorpe deserved a good thrashing but he had to concede that the statutes by which they were governed did not allow for such measures. Mrs Pye, on the other hand, rather favoured a spell of hard labour for Mrs Oglethorpe – preferably in her back garden which had become overgrown since her husband's legs had been amputated and he could no longer attend to the digging.

'Now, let's not be silly,' Mrs Gibbs said. 'I think we should wait to hear about this other offence which Mrs Oglethorpe has committed and we can then deal with both issues together?'

Reluctantly, Sir Willoughby agreed but said, 'Anyway, let's send her off to Northallerton for a spell in a proper jail until then.' Mrs Pye thought that was a capital idea.

'I thought we weren't going to be silly,' Mrs Gibbs said. 'You know we can't do that. I suggest that we bind her over to keep the peace until we hear both charges, unless the police have any objections to that. I'll ask her what she's got to say for herself and if she shows real remorse for the assault and promises to be of good behaviour, then I'll give her one of my stiff lectures.'

Turning to Sir Willoughby she anticipated what he was going to say to her and said that under no circumstances would she allow him to give Mrs Oglethorpe a good talking to, but he could continue to glower at her.

'What can I do, then?' asked a petulant Mrs Pye.

'You can glower as well if you must,' Mrs Gibbs replied. 'But no more nonsense with that black handkerchief of yours, if you please.'

The three magistrates returned to the courtroom.

'We have discussed the situation,' she began as she addressed Mrs Oglethorpe, 'and we will accede to the police request that you face the charges of assaulting two policemen and the theft of a number of diaries at the same time.'

She then turned to PC Wellbeloved and asked if the police had any objection to Mrs Oglethorpe being released from custody until the time of her next court appearance. PC Wellbeloved said that the police would have no objections subject to an assurance on her part of good behaviour and her full cooperation in the police enquiries into the theft of the diaries.

It was a very stiff lecture that Mrs Gibbs delivered to Mrs Oglethorpe. Even Sir Willoughby turned slightly pale. But with her release from custody the day began to turn brighter for Mrs Oglethorpe. Mr Curtis drove her home and indicated that she should lay low until her second court appearance. He said that, subject to her consent, he would speak with the police to see if they might take a more lenient line with her than they would be entitled to follow and he promised to be with her when she was next interviewed by the police.

Seth Womersley had been sitting in the press area of the court when Mrs Oglethorpe had appeared before the magistrates. He was totally unaware that she had even been arrested, as he hadn't bothered to read the court list when he'd rushed into the court at the last minute for his weekly crime reporting session for the *Gazette*. He was torn in two directions as to what he should do. On the one hand he wanted to hear the trial of Alice Oglethorpe and the verdict of the court – and on the other he wanted to get back to tell his Editor that the location of the diaries was now no longer a secret and to expect a call from the police.

Immediately it was clear what the outcome of the hearing was going to be, and he ran all the way back to the *Gazette*.

Chapter 23

The Return of the Diaries

Seth Womersley barged straight into the office of the Editor. With hindsight, this was an unwise move on his part for there, sitting opposite the Editor, was Arkwright Broughton.

'Don't go away,' said the Editor as Seth began his hasty retreat, 'Mr Broughton here has been telling me that nobody returned his phone call to him. Why didn't you do it as I asked you?'

Seth just stood there as though he'd been planted in the ground. Try as he did, words would just not come out of his mouth. But, at last, he did find his tongue.

'I'm afraid that I owe you an apology, Mr Broughton, for not phoning you,' Seth began. 'I did promise the Editor that I'd give you a ring, but I just funked it and the more I put it off the harder it got to do.'

'Well, let's not make it even harder by letting you put your explanations off to me for any longer,' Arkwright Broughton demanded. 'Why did you go pestering my wife in Chiswick? This whole affair is bad enough for us without some spineless little upstart with a pencil and a notebook in his hand poking his nose in.'

'I'm very sorry,' Seth began again. 'I know I should have phoned you and I know that from your point of view that it looks as though we're prying into your affairs. But Old Tom Bones' legacy to Mrs Broughton has caused something of a stir in the Dale and it's our job on the paper to cover the news. I'm very sorry for the trouble I've caused you and Mrs Broughton, but I was only doing my job.'

'You weren't too keen on doing your job when it came to phoning me, were you?' Arkwright replied sarcastically.

Seth could only agree – and his embarrassment was not abated when both the Editor and Arkwright Broughton just continued to stare at him. Seth looked at his feet.

Seth would have dearly liked to tell Arkwright about Mrs Oglethorpe at the court that morning but he knew he had first to give that information to the Editor.

'What is it,' the Editor asked, 'which makes you come tearing into my office without even the courtesy of a knock on the door?'

'It's some bad news I've just heard,' Seth replied, 'and I need your advice urgently.'

Arkwright Broughton stood up to go. 'You'd better get this lad sorted out,' he told the Editor as they shook hands. Seth got no handshake – but he did merit a withering look of frightening proportions from Arkwright.

'Don't you dare ever do that again to me,' the Editor said crossly to Seth. 'We haven't appeared in a very good light with Arkwright Broughton and he's a man of some influence in the Dale. It took me all my time to stop him from going to complain straight to our proprietor.'

'Have the police been to see you yet?' Seth asked.

'No. Why, what have you gone and done now?' asked the Editor, despair writ large across his face.

Seth began by recounting what had happened earlier that morning in the magistrate's court.

'It appears that Mrs Oglethorpe got into a bit of trouble with the police yesterday,' he began. 'They were wanting to ask her whether she had Old Tom Bones' diaries and it seems that she got a bit violent with them. She biffed one copper on the nose and gave the another an almighty kick on his shins. She was then arrested and taken to the police station and it would seem that she's told them that we've got the diaries.'

'Bugger,' said the Editor. 'Where's that damn Mrs Oglethorpe now?'

'The court let her go, so I suppose she's gone home,' Seth said.

'You'd better get to her and find out what she's actually told the police and then get back here as fast as possible.' As a parting shot he added, 'And don't let me down on this one.'

But before Seth could get out of the building he was recalled by the Editor. 'On second thoughts,' he said, 'ring me from the village after you have seen Mrs Oglethorpe and then stay up there and see if anybody saw what went on when she was arrested. It'll make a good front-page story and take the heat off us for buying the diaries from her. Do you know whether she's actually told the police that we'd paid her for the diaries?'

'That didn't come out in court,' Seth replied. 'All that was said was that the police were making enquiries into the theft of some diaries and they asked for her assault charge to be adjourned until both cases could be tried together – but I'd bet my bottom dollar that she did tell them. She looked like a scared rabbit in the court.'

Seth set off for the village and the Editor told his secretary that if the police called to see him she should tell them that he was engaged all morning but to make an appointment for him to see them in the afternoon.

Mrs Oglethorpe was already of a mind not to open the door when she heard footsteps coming from her pathway. She ran upstairs and peered out from behind the bedroom curtains to see who it was calling on her. When she saw it was Seth Womersley she pulled back from the window. The last thing she wanted to do now was to talk to the press about her time in the police cell the previous evening and of her appearance that day in court. She was aware, of course, that Seth knew she'd been in court because she'd seen him there sitting on the press seats. But she wasn't going to go over it all again. At least, not now.

There was another factor which was worrying Alice Oglethorpe. Sooner or later the police would call on the *Gazette* and ask for the diaries. They would probably ask the Editor why he had paid for what he must have known was stolen property, and she knew he would not be best pleased if he eventually found himself in front of the magistrates on a charge of receiving stolen property. There was also the matter of the actual money she had been paid for the diaries. No doubt the *Gazette* would be asking her to pay it back to them – but some worm of a thief had stolen that money from her house together with the few bits of jewellery she possessed.

116

So, all in all, Alice Oglethorpe was not in a mood to receive the press and she ignored Seth's persistent knocking on the door. Only after she had heard Seth retrace his steps down her pathway did she move back downstairs and promptly draw the curtains of her lounge. Better to be behind closed curtains than bars, she thought to herself.

When Seth phoned the Editor and told him that Alice Oglethorpe was refusing to answer her door, the Editor had commented laconically, 'You don't seem to have much success in door to door work, do you?'

Whilst the Editor had not yet received a call from the police, constabulary movement was afoot elsewhere.

PC Wellbeloved phoned Mr Grimsdyke at the bank to report his progress on tracking down the diaries, and he related to him the episode involving the arrest and confession of theft by Mrs Oglethorpe. Whilst he couldn't report that he was yet in possession of the diaries he was confident they would be in his hands later that day.

'What time shall I call round for them?' Mr Grimsdyke asked PC Wellbeloved.

'I'm afraid I won't be able to let you have them until after Mrs Oglethorpe's been tried for their theft,' PC Wellbeloved replied. 'They'll be needed as police evidence against her, but with a bit of luck you'll have them by the weekend.' He promised to let Mr Grimsdyke know immediately when they would be available for him to collect.

Mr Grimsdyke expressed his pleasure and gratitude at the efficiency of the police in resolving the mystery of the missing diaries so quickly. He then phoned Arkwright Broughton with the news. But news travels fast in the Dale and accounts of Mrs Oglethorpe's arrest and confession had already reached Arkwright's ears.

Arkwright had phoned Doris and told her that her ordeal would soon be over, and that in a matter of days she would be able to come home with her head held high. 'I washed some clothes yesterday,' he told Doris with some pride, 'but everything's come out blue.'

Doris laughed and told him not to bother with any more washing and that she would sort things out when she was back home. 'If you need any more clean clothes before I get back, just go out and buy

117

some new ones,' she told her husband.

It had come as a shock to Doris that it was Alice Oglethorpe who had caused so much trouble in the village, and that she had stooped so low as to sell the diaries to the *Gazette*. 'I never particularly liked the woman,' Doris said to Arkwright, 'but I'd never have thought she was that evil.'

'Aye,' replied Arkwright, 'she's a right bad 'un is that one.'

They talked a little while longer of what Doris had been missing in the village, and she had been amused when told of the antics of Constable Pixter. 'It never ceased to amaze me that boy ever got into the police,' she told Arkwright. 'Do you remember the time when he once went fishing in the lake with Daft David and they weren't catching anything. And then they suddenly found their boat in the middle of a shoal of fish and they wanted to know how they could mark the spot for future fishing trips. Daft David had said he would dive overboard and paint a cross on the bottom of the boat and young Pixter said that was a good idea – but then he thought it might not be such a good idea because perhaps they might not get the same boat next time they went out fishing.'

'They were a pair, were those two,' Arkwright said as he remembered the number of times that story had been told in the Cat and Fiddle.

They could both laugh happily now that their ordeal was almost at an end. The stress of the past days and weeks was already beginning to roll off them. The phone call came to an end with Arkwright promising to phone Doris as soon as Mr Grimsdyke had shown him the diaries.

It was late in the afternoon that PC Wellbeloved made his visit to the *Gazette* to meet with its Editor.

'We've been told by Mrs Alice Oglethorpe,' he began, 'that she stole Old Tom Bones' diaries and that she then sold them to you. Can you confirm that?'

The *Gazette* and the police enjoyed a good relationship. In the past, they had both often shared information when it was in the best interest of the community for this to be done, and the Editor was concerned that their relationship should not be damaged by the matter of the diaries. Not that the *Gazette* didn't express an independent and critical line in the matters concerning the police. The paper had published a highly scathing account of Constable Pixter's recent activities at the home of the Blenkins.

'If we were a national newspaper,' the Editor began, 'we would undoubtedly be taking a different line from the one I'm going take now because we don't have the vast resources to test this matter in the courts. Yes, we did buy the diaries from Mrs Oglethorpe and we bought them in good faith. She told us they were hers and we had no reason to doubt her word. After all, she had looked after Old Tom for two decades or thereabouts and it wasn't unreasonable for us to believe that he should have given them to her at some time or other.'

PC Wellbeloved made notes of what the Editor had told him. 'It may be,' he told the Editor, 'that charges could be brought against the *Gazette* for receiving stolen property, but that's not a matter for me to decide. Do you still have the diaries?'

The Editor confirmed that the diaries were being held securely in the newspaper's safe and would remain there pending legal advice as to what parts the *Gazette* could publish.

'I'm afraid that can't be so,' PC Wellbeloved informed the Editor. 'They are material evidence in a case of theft, and I have to ask that you hand them over to me now.'

'I'm prepared to lend them to you,' the Editor replied, 'but not to give them. The *Gazette* bought them in good faith and, as such, they are the property of the paper.'

'I think that'll be a matter for the court to decide,' PC Wellbeloved said. 'I've got a search warrant which I'll use if necessary. I don't suppose you'll be wanting me to turn out all the drawers and files of your offices – who knows what I might just come across once I start looking for the diaries.'

The Editor was impressed by the foresight of the police officer and by the fact that he hadn't approached him in an officious manner by threatening him immediately with the search warrant.

'I'll get the diaries,' the Editor said. 'No need for a search warrant. But I'll want a receipt from you and I'll write on it that the diaries are only being loaned to you for the purpose of your enquiries.'

'By all means,' PC Wellbeloved began, 'write what you like on my receipt, but you'll do that after I've completed it and handed it to you. Your words will not appear on the carbon copy.'

Seth was called into the Editor's office and told to go and fetch the diaries from the safe. It was but a few minutes later that they were transferred to the security of the police station.

PC Wellbeloved phoned Mr Grimsdyke to tell him the diaries had been apprehended, and Mr Grimsdyke in turn phoned Ben Driglington to tell him that the diaries had been recovered from the offices of the *Gazette*. 'I'll not have to take you to court now,' he told Ben Driglington, 'so you can unpack your overnight bag!'

All that now remained to be done was for the trial of Alice Oglethorpe to take place on charges of assault and theft, and for the ownership of the diaries to be determined as vesting in Mr Grimsdyke. With that achieved, the truth – or otherwise – of Doris Broughton having born a child to Old Tom Bones would be determined beyond all doubt.

Chapter 24

The Revelation

With the police having now completed their work, the charge of theft against Mrs Oglethorpe was ready to be heard by the magistrates.

Christina Gibbs JP sighed a deep sigh when she learned that Sir Willoughby Forsythe-Bramley and Mrs Pye would be joining her again on the Bench. 'I wish, just for once, they'd both catch a cold,' she complained to her husband, Norman.

'Get away with you,' he chided his wife. 'You know you like them really. At least they say what they mean and mean what they say. I think you'll find it's only those do-gooders with their 'ology' degrees who think it's fairer for more consideration to be given to the criminals than to the victims. Those two aren't daft – they've both got their feet on the ground. Sir Willoughby may be a bit extreme at times, but I'd sooner follow him into battle than some half-baked sociologist from Luton University covering my back. I sometimes think that you need to take a leaf out of their book when you sit on that Bench.'

'Maybe and maybe not,' Christina replied. And with that the subject was dropped. Christina Gibbs did not take too kindly to it when it was being suggested she was sometimes to soft with criminals. Firm but fair was how she saw herself.

As Alice Oglethorpe walked down her garden path towards where the bus would stop to take her to the small Dale's town which housed the court, she could not help but notice how people crossed the road as they saw her approaching them. She joined the small queue at the bus stop and it was with some courage on her part that she summoned up the strength to say 'Good Morning' to Mrs Finch who was already standing there. Mrs Finch ignored the salutation and turned her back on Alice. By this action, it was brought home to Alice Oglethorpe especially how much the folk of the village now despised her.

Opposite to where she was standing was the lych gate entrance to the small but attractive parish church. Each week a fresh poster appeared on the church notice board sited immediately to the left side of the gate.

Mrs Oglethorpe had not darkened the inside of a church as a communicant member for more years than she cared to remember. But as a child and as a youth she had been a regular church attender.

Having nothing better to do, Alice Oglethorpe read the words on the poster chosen to appear on the church notice board for that week. *When a wicked man turneth away from his wickedness and doth that which is lawful and right, he shall save his soul alive.* Alice immediately recognised the biblical verse as the first of the Sentences of the Scriptures listed at the beginning of the Order for Morning Prayer. Quietly, she recited to herself another of the Sentences frequently used by a vicar at the start of matins which had been imprinted on her mind so many years ago: *The sacrifices of God are a broken spirit: a broken and a contrite heart, O God thou wilt not despise.*

It was not that Mrs Oglethorpe was about to undergo spiritual renewal and be born again, but the words, as words can, brought comfort to her. They reminded her of the security she had enjoyed as a child. For the future, they held out a hope that, following a period of earthly purgatory either in the confines of the village or in Northallerton jail she might, at the last, find herself to be acceptable in the sight of those now so ready to spurn her.

For the remainder of the time waiting for the bus, she just stood quietly in the queue with her head hung low.

In Mr Curtis' car, the journey to the town took just ten minutes. By bus, it was nearer to half an hour as it crept slowly from hamlet to hamlet before eventually trundling into its terminus in a street behind the Market Square. The journey had seemed longer than just thirty minutes that day.

Alice Oglethorpe was met at the entrance to the court by Mr Curtis. Once inside, she asked him would happen that morning.

'As you're going to plead guilty to both charges it will be a simple matter,' he told her. 'Before the magistrates deliver their sentence, I will make a submission on your behalf for leniency, citing your previously unblemished record. You'll be asked if you have anything to say and you'll apologise for assaulting the two policemen and you'll acknowledge how wrong it was of you not only to steal the diaries, but also to sell them to the *Gazette*. In short, you'll grovel like you've never grovelled before and you'll throw yourself on the mercy of the magistrates. I think it's very unlikely that the magistrates will send you to prison, but you'll certainly be bound over to keep the peace and you could be fined for the theft of the diaries.'

And that, indeed, is what happened – bound over to keep the peace for two years and a fine of £150 for the theft. Alice counted her blessings, even if she wasn't too sure where the money was going to come from to pay her fine.

Following delivery of the verdicts, the Editor of the *Gazette* immediately sought out PC Wellbeloved and asked for the return of the diaries.

'I'm afraid that you'll have to see Mr Grimsdyke at the bank if you want them,' the policeman told the Editor. 'The advice we have received is that as Mrs Oglethorpe didn't have a legal title to the diaries so, consequently, neither did you.'

'*Nemo dat quod non habet*,' said Seth to his Editor, remembering the small amount of law he had learned from Mr Driglington when he had consulted him about publication of extracts from the diaries.

Of course, the Editor knew full well the legal position over the diaries having been in such situations before. 'Ah, well,' he said to PC Wellbeloved, 'it was worth a try. I was only bluffing.'

'Just like I was with you,' replied PC Wellbeloved, 'when I said I had a search warrant.' Both men gave each other a wry smile.

'We'll call it a draw, shall we?' the Editor said. The two men shook hands. But in truth, it was two-up for PC Wellbeloved.

Arkwright Broughton bounded up to Mr Grimsdyke and asked when he could start reading the diaries with him. But Mr Grimsdyke had to tell Arkwright that he would have to read them first and then decide what to do with them. He also told Arkwright that it might be necessary to confer with Mr Driglington who had been Old Tom's solicitor – but he promised that he would contact him before any statement was made about Old Tom Bones' child and the claim that Doris was the mother.

It was something of a disappointment to Arkwright that he was not going to be allowed to see the diaries there and then. But he did accept that if what Alice Oglethorpe had been putting about in the village had come from the diaries, then it was only right and proper that Mr Grimsdyke should be the only person to have access to what might be seen as a source document for the expression of all her bile. Arkwright told Mr Grimsdyke that he looked forward to receiving a call from him.

When PC Wellbeloved handed over the diaries, Mr Grimsdyke found they consisted of thirty-five diaries. They were going to involve much reading for him.

He began with the diary covering the period of the year before the birth of the child about whom all the speculation reigned. There were many entries announcing Old Tom's abiding but unreciprocated love of Doris – but nothing saying that they had ever been intimate together. There were scores of entries in which Old Tom recorded his sexual encounters with little Bessie Sidebottom – including the time when Arkwright had caught them at it. The diary also revealed that Old Tom knew that Arkwright had watched them. The first shock for Mr Grimsdyke was where the diary gave out the news that Arkwright, of all people, had fallen from grace with little Bessie in the hayloft. But the date of that entry was such that Arkwright could not have been the father of little Bessie's child.

And then – there it was: *Saw Ben Driglington with little Bessie. A right good mess he made of it – obviously his first time.* Other occasions of spent passions between the two were likewise noted down in the diary. Then, some months later there was mention of an approach from Ben's father offering a very substantial sum if Old Tom accepted little Bessie's child was his, and not that of Ben. The only stipulations to the agreement were that little Bessie was never to be told of the arrangement, and that the child be given the Christian names of James Arkwright. Further entries confirmed that Old Tom had accepted the deal on offer from Ben's father.

But why had Old Tom registered the child with the surname of Ollerenshaw? All that the diaries revealed was Old Tom's eternal love for Doris and his wish that he could give her what she most desired.

Perhaps at the time the baby was born Old Tom had thought that Arkwright and Doris Broughton might be prevailed upon to adopt a child – not any baby but one which had an association with him, albeit somewhat tenuously. But, not too long after the birth, Old Tom had been told that the baby had died and that was the end of that dream.

And then, after so many years, it had been revealed to Old Tom that the child was still alive – but by then it was too late for him to entertain any thoughts about the Broughtons adopting the boy. Perhaps it had been such a story as this that Old Tom had wanted to tell Doris that evening when he had stopped her in the still of the night.

The problem which now faced Mr Grimsdyke was how he was going to give out the news to Ben Driglington that he had a son. And little Bessie would have to be told the full story.

Mr Grimsdyke phoned the offices of Driglington and Co and spoke to Ben. 'I've read through some of the diaries,' he told him, 'and I think we need to meet to discuss a very serious matter I've discovered. Can I come round to see you now?'

'Will it take long?' Ben Driglington asked. 'I've got a client coming to see me in ten minutes and that should take up half an hour. What if we were to meet in an hour?'

It would be a difficult meeting. Mr Grimsdyke made several attempts at rehearsing how he was going to put over to Ben Driglington the bombshell about to be dropped on him. There was no way, he finally decided, but just to come straight out with it and show him what Old Tom Bones had written in his diary – and then just wait and see Ben Driglington's reaction.

Clearly, Ben Driglington would be embarrassed that his first attempts at sexual activity had been recorded for posterity but he would assure Ben that what he had learned from the diaries would go no further than between the two of them. And if Alice Oglethorpe had, by chance, stumbled across those entries in Old Tom's diaries she had not sought to publish them abroad in the unpleasant tittle-tattle in which she had already been engaged in the village. Hopefully, she had not read that far in the diaries before she had sold them to the *Gazette* – and, equally hopefully, neither had anybody at the *Gazette*. With good luck, only he and Ben Driglington would be possessed of the knowledge of what had actually occurred between Ben and little Bessie.

'Now then,' Ben Driglington said to Mr Grimsdyke when at last they met up. 'What magic is there in these diaries which have caused so much trouble and which seem to concern you so?'

'I think you'd better take a look at these entries and see for

Grimsdyke shows Driglington the relevant diary

yourself,' Mr Grimsdyke said to Ben as he handed the diary to him with paper clips attached to the relevant pages.

Ben Driglington read what Old Tom Bones had written and went pale. He picked up his phone and told his secretary that, under no circumstances, was he and Mr Grimsdyke to be interrupted at their meeting.

It was bad enough for Ben to see how his first attempts at lovemaking had been described. He had thought, at the time, he'd done rather well. To learn that his father had connived with Old Tom to cover up the fact that he had begot a son was no less of a shock.

He told Mr Grimsdyke that it was true that he and little Bessie had engaged in acts of intimacy and that little Bessie had told him that he'd got her pregnant. He hadn't believed it could be true because he'd always taken precautions, but she had persisted in claiming he was the father of her child. Matters, he told Mr Grimsdyke, had reached such a pitch that he'd had to tell his father what was going on and his father had told him that he would sort it out. 'As little Bessie stopped bothering me, I just assumed she'd changed her mind. My father and I never talked about the matter again,' Ben said. 'But you know, I should have guessed something odd had been afoot when Fred Dobbs showed me a piece of paper he'd found in Old Tom's papers showing a transfer of funds to him from my father for "special services rendered in connection with Bessie Sidebottom".

'Little Bessie may be a bit weak in the head, but it's my experience that when it comes to knowing who the father of their child is, then women are quite smart. It must have taken some powers of persuasion on your father's part to convince little Bessie that it was Old Tom Bones who was to blame for her condition and not you,' Mr Grimsdyke said. 'Anyway, we can see how Old Tom Bones was persuaded to go along with your father's scheme – it was the money. No wonder Old Tom was able to buy land to increase the size of his farm.'

'I've always wanted a son,' Mr Driglington said, 'and I've had one all the time and never known it. What are we going to do now?'

'Well,' began Mr Grimsdyke, 'we could just say that the diaries show that Old Tom was actually the father and let matters drop at that – but that wouldn't explain why he had said Doris Broughton was the mother of his child. To get over that we could say that Old Tom was so besotted with Doris that he was hoping if he named the child Arkwright then the Broughtons might adopt the boy. But, I'm inclined to the view that unless we tell the truth the speculation won't die down. I think you've just got to grit your teeth and face up to the facts. After all, it happened a long time ago and when people are young these things do happen. It's just unfortunate that when it happened to you society wasn't as liberal as it is today.'

'Where's the lad now?' Ben Driglington asked.

'I don't know that, but some years ago he tried to get in touch with his real parents through his local social services department and they approached Old Tom but he refused to see him. I don't think we should have any trouble in being able to locate him, though,' Mr Grimsdyke said.

'It would be grand if the lad's a solicitor,' Ben Driglington said.

'I think that might put Sue's nose a bit out of joint,' Mr Grimsdyke warned him.

It hadn't occurred to Ben Driglington, until Sue's name was mentioned, that he was going to have some explaining to do to his daughter before the day was out.

'Before we go any further,' Mr Grimsdyke said to Ben Driglington, 'I think we should go and see little Bessie Sidebottom. It will be instructive hear her side of the story.'

The staff of Driglington & Co sensed there was drama in the air when the two men hurried out, and Mr Driglington told his secretary to cancel all his appointments for the day.

It was but a short drive to the small cottage where little Bessie Sidebottom had dwelt all her life. She was surprised to be receiving a visit from two of the town's most prominent citizens.

Once inside the cottage, she offered her two visitors a cup of tea, which they both declined. It was Ben Driglington who spoke first.

'You'll remember that a long time ago you said that you were having my baby and I said you weren't. You were adamant that the baby was mine and then you suddenly stopped making that claim,' Ben said.

Little Bessie looked embarrassed at having this discussed in front of Mr Grimsdyke.

'Don't worry about Mr Grimsdyke hearing about all this. He knows all about it because Old Tom put everything down in his diaries and Mr Grimsdyke has seen what's been written,' Ben Driglington said.

Mr Grimsdyke smiled at little Bessie to try and put her at her ease. 'There's nothing to worry about,' he said, 'but it's rather important that we know the truth of what happened in the past and we do have your best interests at heart. We are not going to do or say anything to anybody which can harm you.'

'Why did you stop saying that I was the father of your baby?' Mr Driglington asked.

'I know people in the village think I'm simple. I know that I'm not quite the same as other folk but I did know you were the father of that baby, even if I was still having it away with Old Tom at the same time as we were doing it together,' little Bessie began. 'But then Old Tom came to see me and he convinced me that he was really the father. I was a lot younger then and you don't stand and fight your corner as you would do if you were older. Anyway, Old Tom convinced me and he said he would get me out of the village to have the baby. When I'd had it he'd said that I should come back and pretend that nothing had ever happened. I went to stay with his aunt and she was good to me and after the baby was a few weeks old she took over and I came back. Then, a bit later Old Tom came to tell me the baby had died and that upset me a lot. I know I should have stayed with the baby and I've never forgiven myself for abandoning the little mite.' Great big tears trickled down little Bessie's lined face and the two stalwart men hardly had a dry eye between them.

When a measure of composure had returned all round, Ben Driglington told little Bessie that he had unwittingly done a great injustice to her. He told her that he really had believed that he was not the father of her child and that it was only that very morning he had discovered the part his father had played in having the child passed off as that of Old Tom's.

And then he told her what Mr Grimsdyke had told him but an hour ago – that her child – their child – was still alive.

Little Bessie wept again and Ben Driglington put his arm round her to comfort her. Mr Grimsdyke went to the kitchen to make a now welcome pot of tea.

'Shall I be able to see my boy?' Bessie asked – and then said, 'Do you think he will want to see me again after I'd just abandoned him so carelessly?'

'*Our* boy,' Mr Driglington corrected her. 'I think that will be very possible for a meeting to take place because some time ago he made an attempt to see Old Tom but he refused to see him. It's time for a new beginning for us all.'

'Did you know that my father paid Old Tom a very considerable sum for him to persuade you that he was the father?' Ben asked little Bessie.

'No,' she said. 'All I got was free board and lodgings with his aunt and my train fare there and back paid for.'

'That was an injustice we'll have to try and put right,' Mr Driglington said.

'With all the rumours which have been circulating I'm going to have to make some statement,' Mr Grimsdyke said to little Bessie. 'And it will have to be told that you and Mr Driglington are the mother and father of the child Old Tom said was his. I'll discuss with Mr Driglington what I'll say and we'll show you the statement before it's published so that you can change any parts which you are not happy with.'

Little Bessie agreed to the way events should proceed and the two men left with her spirits raised high. The child that once was hers, would, by a miracle, be restored to her.

Back at the offices of Driglington & Co, Mr Grimsdyke and Ben Driglington began drafting the statement. They each kept a copy and said they would sleep on it overnight and review it again on the following morning before showing it to little Bessie for her approval. Mr Grimsdyke left Ben Driglington to tell his daughter, Sue, that she had a brother whilst he went back to the bank to telephone Arkwright Broughton.

Chapter 25

Doris Returns

Mr Grimsdyke phoned Arkwright who'd not dared go out least he miss the call.

'Have you read the diaries, then? When can I come round to see them myself?' he asked before Mr Grimsdyke had a chance to say a word.

'It's not that simple a matter,' Mr Grimsdyke told Arkwright. 'There are things in the diaries which I can't disclose to you let alone let anybody else read.' Mr Grimsdyke wondered what Arkwright's reaction would be if he were to see what old Tom Bones had written about his brief encounter with little Bessie Sidebottom. That was a confidence which Mr Grimsdyke was going to have to carry to his grave. But, he was mindful of the way Arkwright had chosen not ever to reveal that his beloved Doris was the cause of the Broughtons not having had a family. And for his loyalty in that connection – despite gratuitous comments being made about his manhood – Mr Grimsdyke was not going to be the one to throw the first stone at Arkwright.

'Whilst I can't let you see the diaries,' Mr Grimsdyke told Arkwright, 'I can now tell you that a statement will be made to the *Gazette* which will be published this weekend. A number of matters have to be cleared with certain individuals before I can tell you what that statement will reveal, but I can tell you with absolute confidence that it will be right for Doris to return to the Dale this Saturday.'

Arkwright tried to press Mr Grimsdyke to tell him more but he

131

was unsuccessful. 'You must wait for the weekend,' was all that he would say.

As soon as the call had ended, Arkwright phoned Doris. He told her of his conversation with Mr Grimsdyke and suggested that she caught the mid-morning train from Kings Cross. That way, he would have the chance to read to her what was in the *Gazette* before she set off and her mind would be at rest. Doris agreed and told him she just could not wait to get back home.

Matters were somewhat more complicated for Ben Driglington. After Mr Grimsdyke had left him he'd called Sue to his office and told her the whole story. It came as a profound shock to her to learn that she had an older brother, and it took some time – and some tears – to pass before she could reconcile herself with what she had just learned.

Ben Driglington had told his daughter of his love for her and that nothing would change that. However, he did have a son and he now had to do right by him. In due course, he told Sue, he hoped to meet that son and it was his hope that the three of them – even though it be late in the day – could reach a happy settlement out of the whole affair. He also told Sue that he owed some duty towards little Bessie for all that she had suffered though his fault – and that of his father – and he asked her to think how he might make some form of amends towards her.

When all had been said, he told Sue that it would perhaps now be appropriate for him to retire from the firm and for her to take over the reins as senior partner at Driglington & Co. For that, Sue was grateful but she was still trying to take in the full measure of the dramatic news which had just been imparted to her.

Since her mother's departure from the family home, Sue and her father had grown very close, and the fact that she was now going to have to share his affection and attention with a stranger would be hard for her to cope with. But for her father's sake she would stand loyally by him as he had stood by her when he had been left alone to look after her. She felt secure knowing that, if her father saw he now had a duty and responsibility to see to his son, then in his sense of responsibility as a father, he would be no less a loving and caring in his sense of care of her.

Little Bessie now had a focus in the eventide of her life. If her son could forgive her for abandoning him, then she would be able to live a more fulfilled life than that for which she had ever dared hope. It might be a little late in the day to join the Mothers' Union but at least she could now openly admit to having the qualification to do so.

Further meetings had taken place between little Bessie, Mr Driglington and Mr Grimsdyke, and a press statement had been agreed. Its form was not quite what the Editor of the *Gazette* had hoped he would obtain from the diaries and for which it had paid a high price but, as he told Seth – 'You win some and you lose some.'

As for Alice Oglethorpe, the paper decided not to prosecute her for the return of the fee they had paid her. She decided, somewhat wisely, to remove herself from the Dale and go and live with her sister in Devon. She moved away a wiser woman. None saw her leave save Mrs Troughton (and Lucifer), and it was Mr Curtis who saw to the sale of her house and removal to Tiverton of its contents.

It was a delighted Doris who returned to a warm welcome in the Dale. Before she had left Chiswick for Kings Cross, Arkwright had read out to her the statement which had appeared in the *Gazette*. On the train journey back she had splashed out on lunch in the dining car. It might have been expensive, but now was the time for a celebration – not for a curled up station sandwich.

On the Monday following her return to the Dale, Doris kept an appointment Arkwright had made for her with Mr Grimsdyke. Doris and Arkwright had discussed over the weekend what she should do with the inheritance Old Tom Bones had left her. The money had been left out of his love for her and there was no doubt that it was rightfully hers. But, as she had told Arkwright, 'We're not used to that type of money, and we've got all we need. Perhaps we could keep a few bob just for a bit of extra security in our old age and to go on a short holiday to celebrate that all this nasty business is over.' Arkwright agreed with her.

Together, they told Mr Grimsdyke of their plans for what to do with the money. A sum should be settled on little Bessie Sidebottom and a part of the estate should go to the Church and for projects in the village. And then, apart from a small amount for themselves, the residue of the estate should be sent to a charity looking after children from broken homes and for children who had been subjected to cruelty.

Mr Grimsdyke listened to their proposals and quietly marvelled at their simplicity and generosity. He felt humbled. He told Arkwright and Doris that he would see to their wishes and would be in touch with them for further instructions when progress had been made giving effect to their dispositions of Old Tom Bones' estate.

Two days later, Arkwright and Doris took their holiday. Nothing grand – just a few days in Blackpool, full of fresh air and fun. At one time, somewhere at the seaside other than on the East Coast (like Scarborough or Bridlington) would have been anathema to Arkwright. But his brief essay into Lancashire when he'd had to fly to America from Manchester Airport had shown him that Lancashire folk weren't quite as bad as he'd previously imagined. Indeed, he'd found Lancashire to be almost as good as Yorkshire.

As Arkwright and Doris explored the Golden Mile followed by a donkey ride on the beach, Mr Grimsdyke pottered in his garden. He collected rubbish for a bonfire but he had no need of a newspaper to set it going.

It was with something of a heavy heart that he set about tearing up Old Toms' diaries. He didn't like destroying the writings of almost half a lifetime of any man, but he and Ben Driglington both thought was the best thing to be done with the diaries was for them to be destroyed. They had come close to ruining Doris Broughton and had seen to the downfall of Alice Oglethorpe. But they had brought happiness to little Bessie Sidebottom and would lead to James Arkwright Driglington being reunited with his parents. On balance, the diaries had brought forth good.

On their arrival back in the Dale, the village had arranged a party for the Broughtons in the village hall. News of it was contained in a letter which they had found on their doormat addressed to them by the vicar. Lying by the side of that letter was another – one carrying American stamps on the envelope. It was a letter from Mary-Lou Jackson letting Arkwright know of her new address so that his solicitor could contact her attorney to pursue his claim for the trauma he'd suffered whilst visiting her ranch.

'Trauma! Trauma!' exclaimed Arkwright to Doris. 'What we suffered out there is nothing to the trials and tribulations we've had to endure these past weeks.' And he gave Doris a smacking big kiss – on both cheeks.